All global publishing rights are held by

Ukiyoto Publishing

Published in 2024

Content Copyright © Manali Desai

ISBN 9789364947589

All rights reserved.

No part of this publication may be reproduced, transmitted, or stored in a retrieval system, in any form by any means, electronic, mechanical, photocopying, recording or otherwise, without the prior permission of the publisher.

The moral rights of the author have been asserted.

This is a work of fiction. Names, characters, businesses, places, events, locales, and incidents are either the products of the author's imagination or used in a fictitious manner. Any resemblance to actual persons, living or dead, or actual events is purely coincidental.

This book is sold subject to the condition that it shall not by way of trade or otherwise, be lent, resold, hired out or otherwise circulated, without the publisher's prior consent, in any form of binding or cover other than that in which it is published.

www.ukiyoto.com

Heartstrings and Harmonies

Manali Desai

Ukiyoto Publishing

Dedication

Dear Husband,

Here goes another Valentine's Day without you admitting,
"You're the best thing that happened to me."
And…
Here's me confessing,
"You're good. But there's still scope for becoming the best."

So, all in all, I'd say
We're better together, at least on most days
On others, well
Let's consider it a win that we succeed at trying not to kill each other

So, all in all, I'd say
We're living the good life, at least on most days
On others, well
Let's accept that we're living the marital bliss (read **blah**) we promised each other

P.S:

Me: 9

You: 2, is it?

(9 = number of books written by Manali.

1/1.5/2 = number of those books read by the husband)

Acknowledgements

On 20th June 2023, per usual, I received the weekly newsletter from Blogchatter. As is the norm since June 2022, the newsletter had two writing prompts, one of which we can choose for writing and submitting a blog post in that particular week.

Now, I've never missed using these prompts for honing my writing skills and to keep my blog active. So, what was different about this particular newsletter then, you ask? Well, you see the first thing was probably the fact that it arrived on my birthday, so maybe it was a sign, who knows? Whatever the case, one of the prompts from that newsletter, *'A short story inspired by your favorite song'*, really tugged at my heartstrings (see what I did there?)

It got the creative wheels in my brain churning and I used the prompt to weave a short story. But the result of the process led to something deeper. It sparked an idea, the result of which, approximately eight months later, is in your hands now.

This book is an outcome of using that prompt, and many others from various sources (including Blogchatter), to weave tales around some of my favourite Hindi songs.

My heartfelt gratitude to Blogchatter, Authoropod Magazine, Unicorn Magazine, Blogaberry CC and The She Saga. It was their writing challenges, prompts and blog hops that worked as an inspiration for this book.

Most of the stories in this collection were first published on my blog. The comments I received on the posts worked as a feedback and encouraged me to convert the stories into a book. So, a big thank you to everyone who read the posts and dropped in lovely comments.

I would not be where I am in my authoring journey without the support of the reading and bookstagram community. Two names on the forefront in this are Sukaina Majeed and Siddhant Agarwal. Without their inputs and contributions in the book promotions, I'd be totally lost. Thank you, you two. Your support means a lot more than I'd ever be able to put into words.

If the cover of this book appealed to you, it was because a group of readers assisted me in deciding which one to pick. I was going crazy trying to zero down on a concept/idea and ended up designing more than a handful covers. This of course led to more confusion than clarity. Without the help of this group, I'd not know which cover looks best. I thank each person in this group from the bottom of my heart. Your enthusiasm was infectious and got my excitement about the book's release to another level. Since a lot of the people from this pool were from the Read With Us book club, I'd like to express my gratitude to its founders and the members. Their prompt willingness to assist me in this task motivated me to go ahead with the idea.

As an author, I did the best I could in terms of language and vocabulary while writing these stories. But the end result wouldn't have the finesse and correctness without the keen eye of Kinnari Desai. Thank you for always being available as my editor and proofreader.

It's been a while since I wrote and put out short fiction. But as I began and went on with the process, I keenly felt the absence of Upasana Arora. She has been that one person to stand firm in my fiction writing journey since my first story collection, ***The Art of Being Grateful & Other Stories.*** This time, though she couldn't be available as much, her inputs were just as valuable. Thank you dear friend, for being someone I can rely on.

One's professional milestones cannot be crossed without the love, support and understanding of the people in their personal life. My thanks and apologies to the husband, my parents, and my in-laws, for bearing with my chaotic moods and work schedules during the making of this book.

Last but not least, thank YOU!

Yes, you. The person reading this. It means a lot that you decided to read this book, when really, you have millions others you could choose from.

That's all, folks.

Let's get to the fun part and here's hoping you enjoy the ride.

P.S: Don't forget to leave a review on Amazon and Goodreads after you're done. It could be two words or ten sentences. It could be good, bad or ugly. It could be one star, two star or five star. Let them all come in.

Contents

Prologue	1
The Rain Falls Pitter Patter	7
In the Free Sky, Let My Dreams Fly Like the Birds	10
It's the Magic of the Season	14
These Threads of Love, Entwined With Your Fingers	18
Sometimes Bitter, Sometimes Sweet	23
Don't Go Just Yet	27
My Companion of This Crazy World	33
It Didn't Happen to Me, Why Did it Happen to You Then?	37
My Heart Has Started to Love You	41
The Coal is Black and Raised by Mountains	44
Our Incomplete Story	51
You're the Reason I Smile and Hum	56
The Moonlight is Raining	58
That's What Life is All About	61
Stand By My Side, My Beloved	63
Oh, Something Strange is Happening	66
The World's Slogan, Stay Vigilant	73
You're the Sunshine	78
With Dreams in My Eyes, I've Left From Home	81
New Colours in Every Moment	85
O Mates, I'm a Wanderer	90
My Shadow Will Follow You	97
This Intoxicating Evening	103
Story of My Journey	107
My Footprints are Your Companion	109
Come Back Home	112

10 years since triple blasts left 27 dead in Mumbai, trial yet to commence	113
This Beautiful Night, Might Not Come Again	115
This Heart Says, Live a Little	118
I Blindly Tread this Path	122
Playlist	127
Other Books by This Author	130
About the Author	138

Prologue

It's love
When they appear out of nowhere like a knight in shining armour to get you home

It's love
When your favourite song becomes their favourite too, and soon after, it transitions into being 'our' song

It's love
When they make your visit to your favourite place, better than you'd imagined

It's love
When they fight tooth and nail with you and the world, to make your life better and to let the world see your beautiful, true self

It's love
When they find a way into your life, and slowly capture your heart, despite your initial misgivings

It's love
When they know just how to woo you, managing to make you smile and forget your grudge against them, within minutes

It's love
When they jump out or onto a moving bus, just to enjoy your company and not leave you alone

It's love
When they want you in their life, no matter how much it hurts, and whether or not you reciprocate their feelings in the same way

It's love
When they remember all the tiny details despite not meeting you for long or not being in your life for many years

It's love
When they help you become a better version of yourself and prepare you best, to help you achieve your dreams and goals

It's love
When their memories and promises, give hope to you, and many others, making everyone believe in the immortality of love

It's love
When they remind you to be your hopeful and optimistic self on days when you feel life's challenges are too much for you to bear

It's love
When they make the time you've spent apart one of the most memorable ones, rather than a painful experience

It's love
When they make you laugh during times when you're both going through a tough phase

It's love
When they think of being reunited with you, during the toughest times in their life even if they can't be with you, and the hope of being together again, keeps them going

It's love
When they accept you back with a smile after a falling out, even when you've caused them heartbreak and hurt

It's love
When they help you realize your purpose, even when it's done under guised affection or by being purposely hurtful

It's love
When they find a way back into your life, just when you need them

It's love
When they provide you with a solution to your problems, when you haven't even asked for their help or shared your problem with them

It's love
When they make you feel welcome in a place you're still finding your footing in and with people you're not familiar with

It's love
When they find a way into your life, when you thought you'd lost them forever or that you never had them to begin with

It's love
When they turn your memories into something that serves as a gentle reminder of the good times you've spent together

It's love
When they leave behind memorabilia that brings generations closer, bridging gaps that some people didn't even know existed

It's love
When their presence is always around you, especially during the tough times, making your journey in that phase, peaceful

It's love
When their words serve as a reminder and give you the strength to survive the tough times

It's love
When they let you go, changing the course of your entire life

It's love
When they welcome you with open arms, simply because you've been through something that they've had to endure too

It's love
When they find a way to help you heal, when they're hurting as much as you are

It's love
When they fulfill your wishes, even in your absence, with or without you by their side

Check out a video rendition of this poem here

P. S.: Come back to these snippets after reading the book. I promise, you'll enjoy and appreciate the poem more.

The Rain Falls Pitter Patter

महफ़िल में कैसे कह दें किसी से
दिल बंध रहा है किस अजनबी से
(How do I tell someone in a room full of people
That my heart is drawn towards a stranger)

Shreyas sang along to the lyrics of the song while driving. He sighed contentedly when the lyrics paused and there was just the melodious music. The tune stirred something deep within his soul. He couldn't help but gaze longingly at the raindrops paving their way down the windshield while waiting at a red light.

When the radio jockey said, "This one is for all the lovers of rain out there. Enjoy the first showers of the season with your beloved...", he hadn't expected it to turn out his own favourite monsoon track.

"The only missing factor here is the 'beloved' Miss Nisha." He addressed the stereo system as if it were the radio jockey and she could hear his response.

Listening to her soothing voice while commuting to work had become a habit. More of an addiction really.

"You should call her *Nasha*[1] and not *Nisha*." Ashwin, his colleague, who often commuted with him to work, had once commented.

"That's quite apt." He had thought to himself but merely smiled as Ashwin patted his shoulder.

"It's your girl signing off now. Remember to tune in at 8 am every day to *Chai Aur Gup Shup*. Goodbye and have a great day, everyone."

Shreyas smiled as he slid his car into its regular spot. Turning the ignition off, he wondered for the umpteenth time how the show was so perfectly timed. On most occasions it ended right when he reached

---
[1] Hindi word meaning addiction/intoxication

his workplace. He whistled as he walked into the office and settled at his desk.

The rest of the workday passed away in a blur. By the time evening came, the morning drizzle had turned into a full-blown torrent. But like everything else about the city of Mumbai, showers like these only meant one more hurdle to overcome in the daily hustle. Rains never meant a full-stop in the Maximum City, they were just a comma; something that brought a lull in the city's pace, never making it stop.

Hence it didn't bother office goers like Shreyas much. The rains were still on as he signed off from work. Tired but still pretty much in high spirits, Shreyas got into the car. Turning the ignition on, he slid it slowly into the lion's mouth viz the never-ending Mumbai traffic. The car stereo's soon reverberated in its interiors.

**जब घुंघरुओं सी बजती हैं बूंदे
अरमाँ हमारे पलके न मूंदे**
(When like ringing anklets, the raindrops fall
My desires refuse to sleep)

Shreyas was surprised at the coincidence. A warm smile spread across his face at the morning's memory. He began to sing along again as he waited at a red signal; a strong sense of déjà vu enveloping him.

Suddenly, a flurry of movement on the left side of the road caught his attention. A girl wearing a red kurta and blue denims was frantically waving at him. Shreyas turned the car towards her once the signal turned green. Rolling down his window, he asked her concernedly, "Hey, what's wrong? Do you need any help?"

"My car has broken down. Can you please drop me at the nearest railway station or a garage. Whatever is convenient for you." She looked flustered, with the raindrops dripping down her face and clothes. Shreyas would have to be literally carved out of stone to say no to her plight.

"Sure, please get in."

She struggled a bit as she closed her umbrella and took a while to get the car door open. Huffing, she landed in the seat next to Shreyas and heaved a sigh so loud that Shreyas couldn't help chuckling.

She threw him an annoyed look which made Shreyas look away. He immediately put the car in motion again and merged in with the ongoing traffic.

रिमझिम गिरे सावन
सुलग-सुलग जाए मन
भीगे आज इस मौसम में
लगी कैसी ये अगन

(The rain falls pitter patter
And enkindles my heart
In this wet weather
What is this fire that rages in me)

"What a coincidence. I played this song just this morning on my show. Hi, I'm Nisha. And you are?"

"Love is so complicated. Why can't God just convey our feelings directly to the one we are meant to be with..."

He smiled amusingly but stayed mute.

"How did you and mom meet?"

A faraway look crossed his face and his eyes ran across the room to the figure in the kitchen. As if sensing his stare, her eyes, which were glued on the pan over the stove, shot up. He winked and the resulting blush was all the motivation he needed.

Chuckling, Shreyas patted his teenage son and began, "I was driving through the heavy rains when..."

Note: This story was inspired by the prompt 'I was driving through the heavy rains when…' and was first published as part of Blogchatter Blog Hop.

In the Free Sky, Let My Dreams Fly Like the Birds

"Ma'am, are you going to get married and leave us too?"

Nita was surprised at such a question from Paridhi, one of her class-five students.

She smiled, and instead of answering, inquired, "What happened Pari? Why such a question?"

"Ma'am, my elder sister got married and left me. I miss her. Why did she leave me?"

Gulping down her chuckle, Nita replied with a straight face, in a consoling manner, "I am sorry your sister had to go. But that's the way of the world Pari. Most girls get married and leave their parents house to live with their new family."

"Will you also leave us when you get married ma'am?" This time it was Anupriya who interjected with the same question.

"I'm not going anywhere." Nita assured her students, who were all suddenly wearing a similar gloomy expression.

"C'mon let's get back to the class now."

ओहो क्या पता जायेंगे कहाँ
खुले हैं जो पल,
कहे ये नज़र
लगता है अब है जागे हम
फ़िक्रें जो थीं, पीछे रेह गयी
निकले उनसे आगे हम

(O ho... who knows where they'll go
When these moments have opened up
Then this sight say that
All the worries that were there, are left behind
We have moved past them)

She clapped in tune to the song while singing it, and soon the children joined her; their anxiety forgotten in the cheerful chorus.

Nita had been a music teacher at a government school for the past three years. She loved her job and the question from the kids today was something that had been playing on her mind too. Her parents were already pressuring her for matrimony and she'd put it off citing one or the other excuse.

"Nita, why can't you come early for once? You know how important today is." Nita's mother, Aruna, complained as soon as she entered home.

Nita shrugged and got busy readying herself.

Let's get this over with. She thought to herself, putting on the saree and blouse her mother had bought specially for this occasion.

"Don't forget the bangles and earrings. I have kept them near the mirror." Aruna shouted from the kitchen.

Holding back a retort, Nita wordlessly did as instructed.

Ting tong!!

The house was bustling soon, as Sunil, Nita's father, opened the door and welcomed the guests.

"Come out when I call your name. Not before that. Carry the tray of tea and snacks with you." her mother directed, before going out from the kitchen and into the hall to join her father.

उड़े.. खुले आसमान में ख़्वाबों के परिंदे
उड़े.. दिल के जहां में ख़्वाबों के परिंदे
(Flying out in the open skies
Flying...are the birds of dreams)

Nita almost dropped the vessel she was holding; wondering whose phone had rung and how it had her favorite song as their ringtone. Before she could ponder further, Nita heard her mother calling out her name. Brushing all other thoughts aside, Nita walked out holding the tray, filled with dread and trepidation.

"This is our daughter, Nita."

"Hello, beta." The elderly man and woman said. Nita smiled and kept the tray on the table. Then she folded her hands in greeting.

"Namaste." She crooned in her softest voice.

The response was immediate. Both the man and woman smiled, pleased with what they saw.

"This is Arun. Our son." The woman said, pointing to the chair on her left. Nita turned in that direction and said "Namaste" again.

Her eyes met his for the first time. Despite her reluctance, she had to admit that he looked good. In fact, better than he did in the grainy photograph her mother had shown her.

"Why don't we let the children talk?" Arun's mother suggested.

"Yes, of course. Nita, take Arun ji to the terrace. You can also show him your gardening results. She has turned our terrace into a small garden." She informed the guests, beaming proudly.

Nita led the way to the terrace, followed by Arun.

"Nita ji. I've been told you love your job." Arun began, after he was done admiring the terrace garden.

"Yes..." Nita hesitated before going on.

उड़े.. खुले आसमान में ख़्वाबों के परिंदे
उड़े.. दिल के जहां में ख़्वाबों के परिंदे

(Flying out in the open skies
Flying…are the birds of dreams)

Nita's eyes jumped to Arun's face in excited bewilderment. He took out his cell phone and cut the call.

"You were saying something Nita ji?"

"I don't want to leave my job." Nita confessed. Her hesitance had dissipated a little after hearing Arun's choice of song for the ringtone.

"I understand of course and I have no issue with you continuing the job after our marriage. We don't live that far from your town and I can always drop and pick you up."

Nita was speechless.

"You do know that I work in your town, right? My office is near to your school and I come here five days a week anyway."

"But..."

"And don't worry about the timing. You can visit your parents if you get free earlier than me. I'll pick you up from here."

Nita had nothing to add to this conversation except look askance at this man. A man she was meeting for the first time, and who seemed to have a solution to all her problems.

"Can you tell me about that ringtone on your phone?" She went with the question which was topmost on her mind.

Arun gave a sheepish smile.

"I have to be honest. This is not the first time I'm seeing you. I came to visit your school last month for some work. You were teaching this song to a class at the time. It was then that I inquired about you and the rest followed, including choosing this song as my ringtone."

Once again, Nita had no verbal response. Her blushing face gave away her feelings though.

Note: This story was inspired by the word prompt 'Kindness' representing the colour peacock green for the Navratri festival. It was first published as part of #AUNavratriBlogHop hosted by Authoropod and Unicorn.

It's the Magic of the Season

**फूलों कलियों की बहारें
चंचल ये हवाओं की पुकारें**
*(The flowers and buds of spring
The calls of these breezes)*

Tanya hummed the lyrics and danced, unbothered about who was watching her. She was finally here in the lap of nature, at the spot she'd been dreaming about; a moment she'd been waiting for, for many years. This monsoon though, she'd finally managed to make time.

**हमको ये इशारों में कहें
हम थम के यहाँ घड़ियाँ गुज़ारें**
*(They are telling us with signs that
We should stop here and spend some moments here)*

She turned around, surprised. She hadn't expected anyone to accompany her in a random singalong. Nonetheless, there he stood; a mischievous smile playing along the edge of his lips. It wasn't quite a full smile, but an amused and challenging one. It was daring her to stop now that she'd been caught in an act she obviously hadn't foreseen an audience for.

Not one to give up, she turned back to nature's bountiful beauty in front of her and went on.

**पहले कभी तो न हमसे
बतियाते थे ऐसे फुलवा**
*(Never before have
The flowers talked with me like this)*

Without turning around, she knew he'd been amused. The chuckle had reached her ears. From the corner of her eyes, she saw his outstretched hands; the singing followed in a few seconds too.

**ये मौसम का जादू है मितवा
न अब दिल पे क़ाबू है मितवा
नैना जिसमें खो गये**

> *दीवाने से हो गये*
> *नज़ारा वो हर सू है मितवा*
> *ये मौसम का जादू है मितवा...*
>
> *(It's the magic of the season, my friend*
> *I have no control on my heart, my friend*
> *My eyes have become lost in which*
> *They have gone crazy in which*
> *That sight is beautiful, my friend*
> *It's the magic of the season, my friend)*

She couldn't help the resulting smile this time. Waving a goodbye without turning around, she continued on her intended path.

"The name is Rahul, by the way. I'm sure you must've heard it."

She laughed in earnest this time. Stopping in her tracks, she turned back and replied, "Shouldn't it be Prem?"

He ran his right hand through the tousled hair and shrugged his shoulders. Not sure how to take the conversation ahead, she started on her path again.

"I can guide you by the way. I've been coming to the Valley of Flowers for the past few years. Not trying to brag, but I do know the best spots."

He sprinted behind her, walking almost in tow but still keeping a few yards between himself and Tanya.

"Best spots to rob me and throw me off the cliff? No thank you!"

"Oh hello! Give the name some credit. Shah Rukh would be offended."

She quirked up her eyebrows, but didn't respond; which he somehow took as a cue to prove his point further.

Shuffling his hand inside his back pocket, he took out his wallet.

"Here is my Aadhar card and it is linked with my PAN card. See it says Rahul Sachdeva and the photo is as bad as I look in person. Do you require OTP authentication too?"

The shriek of laughter that followed was hardly something she could control.

Suddenly, he stopped in his tracks and reached out to grab her shoulder. Irritated, her eyes went to his hand on her body, and he immediately withdrew it.

"I'm sorry." A look of genuine regret crossed his face.

She gave an imperceptible nod which encouraged him to reveal the reason for the stoppage.

"Look there." He pointed to a spot on their left, overlooking the valley.

Tanya's breath caught in her throat. The sight was unlike she'd ever seen before; a scene better than her best dreams; something straight out of a postcard. A stream running through flowers of all kinds, and more colours than one could identify. The source of the stream was a waterfall from a mountain which stood as a magnificent backdrop to the flowing water and the vibrant flowers. Completing the picture perfect frame was the waterfall itself, which fell from the mountain, its jet spray creating a misty aura around the whole field along whose perimeter the butterflies added their own colours.

इनको हम ले के चले हैं
अपने संग अपनी नगरिया
*(I'm taking them along
With me to my countryside)*

She heard the humming close to her ears; this time she didn't mind the proximity. Without looking away from the enchanting arena in front of her, she reached out and grabbed his hand, giving it a slight tug.

है रे संग अन्जाने का
उस पर अन्जान डगरिया
फिर कैसे तुम दूर इतने
संग आ गई मेरे गोरिया
ये मौसम का जादू है मितवा...
*(Oh my, along with a stranger
Even the directions are unknown
Then how did you come so far
Along with me my fair lady
It's the magic of the season...)*

Note: This story was inspired by the word prompt 'Nature & Prosperity' representing the colour green for the Navratri festival. It was first published as part of #AUNavratriBlogHop hosted by Authoropod and Unicorn.

These Threads of Love, Entwined With Your Fingers

2025

तु होगा ज़रा पागल
तूने मुझको है चुना
(*You must be a little mad,*
That you have chosen me..)

Prathmesh hummed the lyrics while rummaging through the kitchen drawers. Finding the spatula he'd been looking for, he used it to toss and turn the omelet over the pan.

He cooked and waited for the others to join him at the breakfast table, reminiscing the first time this song came into his life.

The day that changed his life; for good and, some bad.

2015

"What an amazing movie, right? About time Bollywood learnt to make such good content."

Prathmesh nodded in mute agreement. His mind was elsewhere. Specifically on how the goosebumps on his hands (and even his legs!) hadn't settled even after almost half an hour. His mind kept replaying the moment when, unexpectedly, her head had found its way on to the square of his shoulders. The smell of her hair and the accidental touch of her face to his shoulder, had almost led him to faint.

Somehow he had managed to stay sane throughout the movie, not moving even a bit for the fear of disturbing her comfort. Or was it the fear of losing out on the small victory of finally being so physically close to her? Whatever. The reasons didn't matter. At least not right now.

तु होगा ज़रा पागल
तूने मुझको है चुना

*(You must be a little mad,
That you have chosen me..)*

They were out of the multiplex and in the midst of the maddening Mumbai traffic.

While she hummed the song, also intermittently remarking about how good the movie and the songs were, he tried to hail an auto.

कैसे तूने अनकहा,
तूने अनकहा सब सुना

(How did you listen to everything that was unsaid)

She crooned, reaching for his hand in an attempt to do a little dance along with the singing.

Lost in her world, she missed the oncoming traffic.

"Look out..." Prathmesh grabbed her hand, pulling her to safety.

He registered the look of fear and shock on her face before he felt the jerk. The last thing he remembered was how light he felt as his body flew from one end of the road to the other.

And after that, everything went blank.

2025

"Oooh, this smells delicious. What's cooking, Mr. Husband?" Prathmesh was brought back to the present with her tinkering voice.

Before he could answer, she hugged him from behind. Under the pretext of greeting him, she slyly slid her hand onto the plate and took a bite of the omelet. The moan that escaped her mouth did things to him.

"Well, good morning to you, Mrs. Wife." He chuckled and landed a kiss on her cheek, gently shoving her away.

"Please take a seat and control your urges unless you want Pratim to walk into a live X-rated movie."

"My urges, huh?" She teased while kissing and biting his ear. He groaned, reluctantly letting go of her hand as she laughed and made herself comfortable at the dining chair.

> *कैसे तूने अनकहा,*
> *तूने अनकहा सब सुना*
> (How did you listen to everything that was unsaid)

Prathmesh hummed and this time it was Priti who was tugged down the memory lane.

2018

"Devil, devil" The little kid pointed at something and ducked behind his mother.

"What's wrong with his face? He looks like a beast!" The mother inquired her husband loudly, while dragging her son away quickly, hiding his face in her pallu.

Priti tightened her grip on his hand. Determinedly, she turned to the retrieving family and shouted out angrily, "Nothing is wrong with his face! It's your sight and thinking that's the beast."

"Let it be, Priti." He looked apologetically at the family and dragged her away from them quickly.

"Enough of this nonsense. We're getting your surgery done at the earliest."

"Priti, you know what the doctors said. Plus, the expenses."

"I don't care, we'll go abroad. I'll manage the finances."

> *तु होगा ज़रा पागल*
> *तूने मुझको है चुना*
> (You must be a little mad,
> That you have chosen me..)

He started humming. The effect was instant. Her frown turned into a smile and looping her hand through his elbow, they walked on.

"Don't laugh or avoid the answer this time, okay?"

He sighed, almost as if he knew what was coming.

"Priti, your life will be..."

"I have already booked the venue."

He coughed. But before he could interrupt, she cut him off, "We are getting married."

Shrugging his shoulders, he shook his head defeatedly.

> तु होगा ज़रा पागल
> तूने मुझको है चुना
> *(You must be a little mad,*
> *That you have chosen me..)*

He hummed and she chuckled as they walked on, hand in hand.

2025

"Mommy, mommy..."

They looked at each other in panic and rushed into the bedroom opposite the kitchen.

Their five-year-old son, Pratim, had a photograph clutched in his tiny hands. Tears streamed down his little face as he looked at the photo with fear and curiosity.

Priti ran to his bed and enveloped him in a hug, while Prathmesh took the photograph from Pratim's hand.

"The Beauty and The Beast." Prathmesh read out the caption below the photo loudly.

"Who is that beast with you in the photo mommy?"

"That is not a beast, Pratim. That's your father."

Pratim looked at the person in the photo and then at his father, clearly confused.

"Let me tell you a story, darling." Priti began.

Prathmesh settled down in the bed too, taking hold of Pratim's hand.

"It's your parent's version of The Beauty and The Beast..." He chuckled and added.

Priti smiled and continued narrating their story. The story of how they became lovers from best friends, and how an accident changed their lives. And most importantly, how, one Beauty's determination, restored a Beast into a human.

तु होगा ज़रा पागल
तूने मुझको है चुना
कैसे तूने अनकहा,
तूने अनकहा सब सुना
*(You must be a little mad,
That you have chosen me..
How did you listen to everything that was unsaid)*

Prathmesh added his bit to their story, humming the song that started it all.

Note: This story was inspired by the prompt 'Rewrite Beauty and the Beast with your twist' and was first published as part of Blogchatter Blog Hop.

Sometimes Bitter, Sometimes Sweet

कभी नीम नीम
कभी शहद शहद
कभी नरम नरम
कभी सख्त
मोरा पिया...
(Sometimes bitter
Sometimes sweet
Sometimes soft
Sometimes hard
My beloved is like that)

"*मोरा पिया* (my beloved)...*मोरा पिया* (my beloved)...ohhhh," Mitali stopped, realizing that the song had been turned off. She looked around, and almost choked on the next lines. She'd been caught in quite an embarrassing stance; a ladle in one hand, and her other hand and left foot in the air.

Someone coughed, and she quickly got her hands and foot in place, adjusting her clothes too.

"Mitali, these are my colleagues. They wanted to check out our new house." Nitin explained, then walked over to her and placed a comforting hand around her shoulders.

Mitali relaxed instantly and remembered her manners.

"Hello. Welcome. Please take a seat."

Mitali escorted the guests from the kitchen door to the sofa in the hall. While Nitin served them water, she excused herself and got busy in the kitchen again.

"A little heads up would've been nice." She snarled at Nitin when he came into the kitchen to drop off the glasses.

"Sorry, Mitu. I casually mentioned that you're making samosas today and they invited themselves. What am I to do when your samosas are so popular? Plus, it's the last working day before the Diwali break, I just couldn't refuse. " Nitin sounded defeated and the look on his face was enough to melt Mitali.

She smiled reluctantly and shook her head. Nitin gave her a quick hug, whispering in her ear, "Let's continue that performance later, by the way." He pinched the exposed skin on her waist and moved out of the kitchen before she could react.

नज़रों के तीर
मे बसा है प्यार
जब भी चला है वो दिल के पार
लज्जा से मैरे रे ये जिया

(There's love
In the arrow of his eyes
Whenever it pierces through my heart
It has dies from shyness

Mitali heard him humming the song as he made his way to join the guests.

"Bhabhi, you have to teach Ragini how to make them so well." Vikas said, munching on a samosa.

All the guests were served tea, samosas and a few other snacks. As expected, nobody even looked at the other offerings and the samosas were getting gobbled faster than a hungry cat chasing a tired mouse.

"I'd love to. Why don't you two come home for Diwali?" Mitali beamed at Vikas's praise and offered.

Vikas nodded absently, completely engrossed in savoring the snack.

"But here, the secret ingredient isn't in the food. Is it Mitali?" Nitin revealed, a smug expression on his face. Mitali visibly turned pink and gave him a warning look.

"Oh, we must know now." Vikas prodded, giving a playful nudge to Nitin.

"What's the story here?" A couple of other guests chimed in.

All the guests put down their samosa, which was a momentous feat in itself. They looked from Nitin to Mitali expectantly, literally holding on to the edge of their seats, awaiting for either of them to reveal further.

"It's nothing as such, please..." Mitali began, clearly shy.

Unanimously, everyone's heads turned in Nitin's direction.

"It was the first dish by Master Chef Mitali I had the privilege to taste..." Nitin revealed.

"Did she make them for you at your first meeting?" Vikas queried.

"Hardly," Nitin chuckled, and landed a slap on Vikas's shoulder. "Ours is not an arranged marriage like yours, mister."

Nitin then looked at Mitali, winked conspiratorially and went on, "Back then, Mitali was running a cloud kitchen in partnership with some food delivery apps. That's how I first came upon the samosas too. Of course I fell in love with the samosa the minute I tasted it. And then it became my life's purpose to find the person who had made them. I found her business page on socials, and stalked and DMed the page relentlessly." He sighed, taking a brief pause.

Everyone waited with bated breath.

"Well, continue, I want to get back to my samosa!" Vikas sounded impatient and picked up his half-eaten piece.

Both Nitin and Mitali let out a chuckle, and then Nitin continued, "Mitali being an introvert and camera-shy person, there were no photographs of her anywhere. Only her hands, her voice overs and her dishes made an appearance on the business page feed. One day she shared a samosa making reel, with the song *कभी नीम नीम कभी शहद शहद*, explaining that samosas are like the lyrics of the song; sometimes best accompanied with bitter and spicy chutneys, sometimes with sweet drinks. They're either soft or hard, depending on their filling."

"That was the moment he lost patience and knew he had to talk to me." All faces turned towards Mitali as she continued. "He did the unthinkable and gave me a call from the social media page. I was in the middle of something and instead of cutting it, I mistakenly answered the call. I heard *कभी नीम नीम कभी शहद शहद* (sometimes bitter, sometimes *sweet)* in the background and this random guy, I'd never spoken to before, explaining me why he is just like my samosas and the song, and why I should give him a chance. I checked the ID and recognized him as the one who'd been commenting on my posts and DMing incessantly for the past couple of months. Despite myself, I laughed. Though my logical mind said this is probably how most people get murdered, I began talking to him, little by little. The rest as they say... is history."

"What was it about the song though?"

"Why कभी नीम नीम कभी शहद शहद *(sometimes bitter, sometimes sweet)*?"

A couple of the guests were curious to know further.

This time, Mitali looked at Nitin and winked conspiratorially, before revealing, "Apparently, it was the song that he'd always wanted the girl he fell in love with, to dedicate to him."

"So now, whenever the song is playing, I know Samosas are coming." Nitin laughed and the others joined in, while digging into the yummy snack.

Note: This story was inspired by the word prompt 'Food' and was first published as part of Blogaberry CC.

Don't Go Just Yet

हवा ज़रा महक तो ले,
नज़र ज़रा बहक तो ले
ये शाम ढल तो ले ज़रा,
ये दिल सम्भल तो ले ज़रा
(Let the air get fragrant
At least divert your attention a bit
Let this evening fade away
Let this heart get a bit steady)

"**मैं थोड़ी देर जी तो लूँ, नशे के घूँट पी तो लूँ**.....(Let me live a little longer, let me take a sip of intoxication)" My crooning continued for a few seconds before I realized Mohammed Rafi and Asha Bhosle had stopped filling my ears. Not for the first time, I understood why people's faces turned cringey around me when I sang. Smiling, I turned around to see what had caused the break in my evening self-serenading routine.

Kritika, my wife, stood with the remote control in her hand. Why had she paused the song though? The reason could be anything ranging from an impending tsunami to a cockroach sighting. One can never tell. Hey, ask any husband!

Anyway, I looked at her inquiringly, while she continued to stare at me. Again, it took me some time to apprehend that it wasn't just *a stare*. Oh yeah, this was a glower. Impending tsunami it is then, I guess. I braced myself for the calamity while Kritika waved something around. My eyes fell on the document she was holding in her right hand; left one deftly still placed on her hip.

Oops! Busted.

"I was cleaning my cluttered desk and found the document beneath a pile of papers. Care to explain?"

Uh-oh.

Yeah, things were not just bad. They were worse. That tone was last heard in circa 1995 and I was not even on the receiving end then. You see, Kritika was pregnant with our firstborn, Karun. The due date was still two weeks away. But her water broke when we were at my firm's year-end party. A group of people were blocking the exit and Kritika lost it. A loud and angry tirade on civic behavior and social responsibility followed, which went on till I had to point out that the people had moved and the path for us was clear. Yep, *that tone!*

I gulped, trying to frame an explanation that would lead to least damage.

"I asked you something, Kunal."

"Well, you know Karun and Disha have been together for three years now..." I began, falteringly.

"How long have you known?"

"I don't remember." I was deliberately vague as I mentally kicked myself for using the home printer to peruse the document Karun had shared.

"They wanted my opinion, seeing how I am in the same field and all."

Silence.

"It was meant to be a surprise for everyone else I guess..." I tried to salvage the situation.

She let out a 'hmmph' and turned around, ready to exit.

मैं थोड़ी देर जी तो लूँ
नशे के घूँट पी तो लूँ
अभी तो कुछ कहा नहीं
अभी तो कुछ सुना नहीं
अभी ना जाओ छोड़कर...

(Let me live a little longer
Let me take a sip of intoxication
You haven't said anything yet
You haven't heard anything yet
So don't leave just yet)

The song back on, I serenaded my better-half, embracing her from behind and twirling her around.

"I am sorry." I whispered into her ear as we slow-danced in each other's arms.

A hint of a smile showed, but her lips were still pursed.

"Well, alright. But next time someone in the family buys a house, you let me know. Or you better pray they have room for you in that house."

"That's hardly fair. The kids never come to me. Let me have one win at least." This time I moved away, a bit put off.

बुरा न मानो बात का, ये प्यार है गिला नहीं
हाँ, यही कहोगे तुम सदा, के दिल अभी भरा नहीं
हाँ, दिल अभी भरा नहीं, नहीं नहीं नहीं नहीं

(Don't feel bad about it, this is love not a grudge
Yes, you will always this, the heart is not full yet
Yes, the heart is not full yet, no way, no way, no way, no way)

Kritika serenaded and twirled me around.

In a few seconds, Rafi and Asha's voices were drowned amidst an off-key duet mingled with laughs.

Note: This story was inspired by the prompt 'I was cleaning my cluttered desk and found the document beneath a pile of papers' and was first published as part of Blogchatter Blog Hop.

My Companion of This Crazy World

इस बेढंगी दुनिया के संगी हम ना होते यारा
अपनी तो यारी अतरंगी है रे
कर बेरंगी शामें हुड़दंगी मस्त मलंगी यारा
अपनी तो यारी अतरंगी है रे

(O my companion of this clumsy world,
had we not been friends,
our friendship is colourful..
make these colourless evenings
full of fun, carefree, O friend..
our friendship is colorful..
colourful.. O yeah..)

The ringtone cut through the conversation and the youngest Varma stopped midway with her tirade.

"Hey, Naina. Listen, I'm having dinner. I'll call you in a while, unless Arjun doesn't kill me. You know who the prime suspect would be though now. Bye!"

"Naina this. Naina that! I hope this new friend of yours isn't imaginary. A year ago, you were convinced your teddy bear was a person who was responding to your statements." Arjun Varma teased his little sister, Sujata Varma, as soon as she was off the phone.

She had recently entered college and nobody was surprised when she returned home dejected on her first day. Being a bookworm, homebody, and an introvert, made human interactions seem more complicated than algebra for Sujata. As family members, all the other Varmas could do was listen with empathetic ears and give her the hope that things would get better in the coming days.

The saga, however, continued for almost a month. So much so that one day Sujata stomped into the house and demanded, "I want to drop out of this college and try for another one."

Ashok, Sujata and Arjun's father, was strictly against giving in to such irrational demands. On his wife Sumitra's constant cajoling (some might call it nagging!), he finally agreed to speak with the college principal in a couple of days and get Sujata's admission withdrawn.

Before that day could come though, Sujata began singing an altogether different tune.

She had found a friend in Naina Sabharwal. The girls were like apples and oranges, having nothing in common. Right from their family backgrounds and dressing styles, to their popularity in college, the two differed in everything. Sujata and Naina becoming best friends was an unlikely scenario; similar to spotting a clean pair of white shoes on a rainy day (you'll appreciate this joke later in the story, I promise).

Arjun's doubt at his younger sibling's talks could be understandable, given how gullible Sujata was. Plus, she had been talking about Naina for ten minutes straight to Ashok's simple question, "How is college treating you now?"

The way their daughter went on about this 'Naina' girl, a sliver of doubt crept up in Ashok and Sumitra's minds as well. What with Sujata making Naina sound like some exotic, unbelievable creature. After all, being in Sujata's good books was no easy feat.

But being concerned parents, Ashok and Sumitra didn't vocalize their thoughts the way Arjun did.

Sujata stuck her tongue out and blew a raspberry in response to Arjun's statement. A unanimous laughter erupted from the mouths of the other three Varmas. It was more a sign of relief than anything else. The four Varmas were seated at the dining table for dinner and after a long time the mood was light.

"Here! See for yourself." Sujata thrust out her hand, showing a photograph on her phone.

"This is right after our first meeting." She gushed, looking fondly at the photo in question. On the screen, two girls, with wet hair and water droplets on their faces, were grinning from ear to ear. It was clear that their smiles were the follow-up of a round of laughs.

She scrolled and moved to the next photo saying, "We took this one on a rainy day when we decided to bunk the lecture and have a cup of cutting chai at the roadside tea stall outside our college."

Two hands holding out a cup of tea each were visible in this one.

"How did you two meet?" Arjun asked the question that was on everyone's minds.

"It's a funny story actually. Another rainy day anecdote. As you know, I take the bus from Malad station for college. But Naina is dropped off by their driver in one of their many luxury cars. It's a different one every day of the week."

The other Varmas nodded; now completely invested in this story.

"The car that was supposed to drop Naina that day broke down because of the flooding. Its tires got stuck in one of the potholes and there was no time to wait for the car to get out, as Naina was getting late."

"This is beginning to sound a lot like a romcom..." Arjun butted in.

"Not now, Arjun."

"Shhhh..."

Ashok and Sumitra burst out together and it was Sujata's cue to go on.

"I knew her of course. Because she's all over the college; actively participating in everything inside and outside the class. I looked out of my bus window and saw her getting drenched in the rain on the sidewalk." She paused a bit, chuckling, and continued, "I still remember how forlorn she looked, like Santa had denied her the gift she'd wanted for Christmas. Anyway, our eyes met for a few brief seconds and I saw a flicker of recognition on her face, followed by relief. I did wonder how the popular girl knew the class recluse. But when she started running behind the bus like a possessed woman, I lost the thread of any sane thoughts too. I immediately jumped from my seat and ran to the door."

"Well, c'mon! Really, the story is writing itself now..."

The threatening looks from his parents had Arjun gulp down the rest of his comment.

"Anyway, I stretched out my hand to help her get in and we've been BFFs ever since."

Turning to Arjun she added, "It's not a romcom, but maybe our story will start a new genre, friendcom?"

Another round of laughter followed, this time from four mouths; filling up the Varma household with hopes of better days.

Note: This story was inspired by the prompt 'I looked out of the window and our eyes met' and was first published as part of Blogchatter Blog Hop.

It Didn't Happen to Me, Why Did it Happen to You Then?

"Shut up! That's not true!" Binal snarled, arms crossed defiantly. The pout that Arvind had come to associate with such outbursts, followed in about five seconds.

"Okay, sorry. What would you like to have then?" Arvind asked, suppressing his chuckle.

Arvind had assumed that his best friend, as was her habit, would be ordering a cheddar veggie sandwich and a cold coffee. Adding to this assumption, he made the grave mistake of making a snide remark, "Do I even need to ask what you'd be having, Binu? You are as predictable as the social media comments on a couple pic. Rab ne bana di jodi[2]. Made for each other. Looking good together. A pair made in heaven. Cutest couple. And my favorite. Couple goals. Uff!"

She wanted to laugh (well, of course he was right about both things!) but just to prove him wrong, decided to put him in his place. Following Arvind's lackadaisical apology, she snatched the menu from Arvind. With her face scrunched up in annoyance and determination, she pored over the offerings.

"I'll have a cheesy toast and a caramel latte."

Arvind nodded, quickly turning his face away. The pursed lips didn't miss Binal's eyes though. She knew him too well, and sometimes it was a curse. Now, she'd have to endure not one but two food items which weren't her preferred ones.

The things we do for love. The thought crossed her mind, not for the first time since the last few months.

Soon, they took their seats at one of the empty tables.

---

[2] A Hindi phrase which translates A Match made in heaven/A match created by the Almighty himself

मिलना नहीं है मुमकिन
इतना बताओ लेकिन
हम फिर मिले क्यूँ हैं
तुझको बुला ना पाउन
तुझको भुला ना पाउन
यह सिलसिले क्यूँ हैं
सब कुछ वही है
पर कुछ कमी है
तेरी आहटें नहीं है

(It's not possible for us to be together,
Tell me this then
Why did we have to get together
I can't call you,
I can't forget you,
Why is it so?
Everything is the same,
But something is missing..
The sound of your being isn't there..)

The song and its lyrics turned the mood sombre instantly. Binal averted her eyes, lest the tears that had sprung up decided to make themselves another unwanted dish on the table.

"Binu, can we talk about it, please?" Arvind broke the awkward and stretched silence. He reached out to grab Binal's hand, but she withdrew it before he could do so.

"There's nothing to talk about, Arvind. I decided what was best for me. And sometimes, that's not selfish."

"What about me though? What about our friendship? This isn't my fault so why am I being punished?"

Their order arrived right then. Giving them both a respite from a conversation none of them would ever feel ready to have.

"Enjoy your food and drinks, ma'am and sir." The waiter wished them, and took his leave. The sight of the cheesy toast and caramel latte made Binal frown, adding to her frustration.

"Arvind, it's not fair of you to say that. I'm feeling punished as well as guilty. You have no idea what it's like to live under the same roof as the person you love and not be able to love them as you want. Or worse, not having them love you the way you love them. That's why I decided to move out. And, let's not get into comparisons, please. I felt something, and you didn't. That's it."

Sighing, she took a piece of sandwich and reluctantly stuffed it in her mouth. It wasn't all that bad, so that was some respite from the turmoil she felt within.

Pretending to enjoy the sandwich, Binal took in the cafe's patrons and interiors. With a pang, she recalled the moment when she had realized her feelings for Arvind went beyond friendship. It was right here in this very cafe a couple of months ago. Arvind had reached out to an elderly woman for offering help in placing her order. Clearly it was the older woman's first outing at such a place and she didn't understand any of the items on the menu. She'd always had a soft spot for Arvind in her heart. But it was at that moment the tunes of her heart ran across her entire being.

"Do you remember the last time we were here?" Arvind's question brought her back to the present.

She merely nodded, not wanting to divulge into the details of how and why she remembered those moments.

"That woman is now my Facebook friend and wants me to meet her daughter. Playing matchmaker and all." Arvind went on, oblivious to the havoc this statement caused in Binal's heart.

"You should take up the offer. Maybe someone will finally be able to steal your heart." Binal chuckled and remarked, masking her pain.

Arvind observed her closely for a few seconds, as if gauging whether Binal was serious. Then nodding his head, relented, "Yeah, maybe I will bring her to this place and tell her how it started right here."

Binal joined him in the laughter this time, happy for her best friend.

At least someone's love story will find a happy ending here, she thought to herself.

A part of her also wondered how one place, one person, and even one moment, could mean and lead to so many different scenarios in different people's lives.

"How's your non-regular order, by the way?" Arvind asked.

"I prefer to be predictable." She answered reluctantly, rolling her eyes.

"I knew it!"

The two friends laughed at each other's familiarity, savoring the joy of meeting after a long time.

Soon enough, the mood turned light again, putting her and Arvind right back in their comfort zones. For now, she would take that over her unrequited feelings; the ones she was sure she'd learn how to deal with, over time.

Note: This story was inspired by the word prompt 'Comparison' and was first published as part of Blogaberry CC.

My Heart Has Started to Love You

आ जा ओ मेरी जान
मेरे दिल का जहाँ
माँगे तेरी ख़बर
ढूनदे तेरा निशान
(Come to me my love
Into the world of my heart
It wants to hear about you
And it's searching for your traces)

Eyes closed, he was humming the song softly, lost in the magic of its lyrics, when he felt a soft tap on his shoulder.

"Will it be coffee with two sugars, Mr. Aditya Ahuja?"

He nodded, eyebrows shooting up in curiosity.

Do they train the airline staff to memorize the passengers' names too these days? He wondered.

The doe-eyed, fair-complexioned attendant probably gauged his inquisitiveness. But instead of curbing it, she took it up a notch.

"Mr. Ahuja. I also know which school you passed out from and your favorite movie. I am pretty sure that I can predict the song you were listening to right now. Oh! And I can make a bowl of Maggi noodles with the precise amount of gravy you prefer."

Aditya's mouth was left hanging open.

What is this sorcery? Is this some voodoo plus AI combo I haven't got a memo on? He almost blurted out his thoughts this time. But was stopped short as the hostess handed him his coffee and the standard snack. Her tag read Shreya Bakshi.

Quickly he jogged his memory but nobody named Shreya came up in his mind.

Before he could get back his bearings, the woman had already moved along the aisle to the next passenger.

Sure, she was pretty and the face did look oddly familiar. But he had never known a Shreya in his life as far as he could remember.

The rest of the flight, he kept thinking about this eerie encounter; trying to place Shreya Bakshi's face to all the women he knew, right from the ones he had studied or worked with, to the ones he had dated, even briefly. But it was all in vain.

When it was time to deboard, he deliberately took his time, making sure he was one of the last ones out.

Miss Shreya had probably anticipated this too. Before he could engage with her, she handed him a business card and wished him a good day.

Like most cards, this one too bore her name, designation and professional contact details. He turned it over and suddenly felt the air around him whistling loudly.

गली-गली घूम दिल तुझे ढूनदे
गली-गली घूम दिल तुझे ढूनदे
तेरे बिन तरसे नयन
(My heart roams in the streets and searches for you
My eyes are yearning to see you)

Beneath the lyrics in smaller handwriting a name had been written inside a friendship band doodle. *Shreyas Bakshi.*

A flashback from thirteen years ago. The school playground.

A group of lads besieging a boy from their class. A boy who was often cornered, bullied and teased for being soft. A boy who had always been kind to him. A boy who had always seemed lost. A boy he had stood up for that day, and on many occasions after that. A boy he'd since become best friends with. A boy whose music interests had been shockingly similar to his.

A boy who had gone AWOL after school.

"Well done, Miss Shreya. Wanna meet and catch up over coffee?" Aditya smiled and typed in a message as he hailed a taxi and departed from the airport.

Note: This story was inspired by the word prompt 'Transformation' representing the colour grey for the Navratri festival. It was first published as part of #AUNavratriBlogHop hosted by Authoropod and Unicorn.

The Coal is Black and Raised by Mountains

उलझे क्यूँ पैरों में ये ख़्वाब
क़दमों से रेशम खींच दे
पीछे कुछ ना आगे का हिसाब
इस पल की क्यारी सींच दे
(Why are your dreams entwined around your feet
Release them like silk from your steps
Don't think about your past or the future
Just focus on weaving your present)

"Alexa, stop!" Samip paused the song, shaking his head as he looked at Pranav.

"Do you know the meaning of these words?" Pranav's nonchalant shrug indicated his ignorance and disinterest.

"Have you seen the movie at least?"

This time, the young lad gave an enthusiastic nod, "It's one of my favourite sports movies."

"And why is that?" Samip prodded his protégé.

"It's inspiring because it shows how a man can excel even in the worst conditions." Pranav pondered and added, "I think it was one of the first reasons I took an interest in athletics myself."

"That's wonderful, Pranav. But reel life and real life are different. I hope you realize that."

"All I know is that I love sports and am ready to give my hundred percent."

"That makes my job as your coach easier, son. Now back to this song. The lyrics we paused at, convey that you shouldn't let your dreams get entwined around your feet but release them like silk and take the next step forward."

Seeing the blank look on Pranav's face, Samip pressed, "For any sport, muscle strength is of utmost importance. That includes arms and legs." Samip did a flip and roll to make his point about flexibility and how vital it was for Pranav's future in any sport.

Impressed, Pranav imitated Samip's moves, and ended up falling flat on his back.

"That's exactly what we need to work on. You're concentrating on the end goal. You see yourself excelling at sports but you don't want to focus on getting fit and flexible first." Samip held out his hand, helping Pranav up.

"So, what should I do, sir?"

"Begin small," Samip touched the knee cap of Pranav's left foot. "Learn to free your body parts and the rigid muscles." He then touched Samip's right hand elbow.

"These parts need to be worked on. This'll also help us decide which sport to focus on. Do you have a preference?"

"I do enjoy badminton. But I'm open to exploring other sports."

"That's good." Samip thumped Pranav's back. "Let's begin again, shall we? Alexa play!"

आग जुबां पे रख दे
फिर चोट के होठ भिगायेंगे
घाव गुनगुनायेंगे
तेरे दर्द गीत बन जायेंगे

(Keep a flame burning on your tongue
Then even your burning lips will sing
Your wounds will hum
Your pain will turn to songs)

The song played on loop as the coach and his new student worked on loosening up Pranav's various body parts. Neither realized when hours went by.

"Alexa, stop."

Their workout was interrupted by Samip's wife, Suman, who walked in with Pranav's mother, Heena.

"Sorry to end the party boys. Time's up."

"Cinderella has to put up her shoes."

The two women chuckled at their own jokes and dragged Samip and Pranav out of the garage, which Samip had converted into a makeshift training room.

Bidding farewell, Heena and Pranav made their way to their car.

"So, how was it?" Heena asked once they were seated and enroute.

"He's something else. You know, we didn't play any sports at all." Pranav said, with a confused smile.

"Hmm, I hope he knows what he's doing. You insisted on him though so if he fails, it's on you, kid." Heena gave her tween son a playful nudge in the ribs.

"Mom, stop!"

"Tell me why Samip though?"

Pranav went on to justify his choice, a bit defensively.

"He was kicked out as our school sports coach before I could start training under him more extensively. It was an unfair dismissal and the senior boys stopped playing any sport for six months. I was just curious to know why he was so popular. Of course the fact that the school won every sports event with him as the head coach was another reason."

"How do you know it was an unfair dismissal?"

"Samip sir was always an impartial teacher. One of the entitled kids took it the wrong way when sir benched him for an entire season during an interschool sports event, which the school ended up winning. The kid's and parents' egos were hurt. The parents were on the PTA and to save their snotty noses, they concocted a story about how sir chose students based on bribes. They even planted gifts and cash in his bag to prove their case. It was quite ugly and sad."

Heena let out a low whistle before responding.

"That's definitely unfair. So, he runs his own coaching center now?"

"That's what I heard. And I could be one of his first proteges; a chance I did not want to miss out on since my love for Badminton and Volleyball has grown."

Heena ruffled her son's hair saying, "Well, if what you say is true, I see a Wall of Honour in the making for Mr. Pranav Mehta."

The determination on the young boy's face made both mother and son look to the future with renewed vigour.

---

5 years later

ज़िन्दा हैं तो प्याला पुरा भर ले
कंचा फूटे चूरा कांच कर ले
ज़िन्दगी का ये घड़ा ले
एक सांस में चढ़ा ले
हिचकियों में क्या है मरना
पूरा मर ले...

(If you're alive then fill your glass up to the brim
If the glass breaks, then turn the pieces into another glass
Take this pot of life
And drink it all up in one breath
Why should we die with hiccups
It's better to die completely)

The lyrics of the song reverberated through the stadium as the booming voice of the commentator announced the final results.

"And, for the gold, we have our youngest in the Under-19, Mr. Pranav Mehta. Give it up for this promising young man."

Pranav walked up to the dais, taking his place atop the number one spot. He then bowed down to accept the gold medal which was placed around his neck by the State Sports Minister.

कोयला काला है
चट्टानों पे पाला
अन्दर काला बाहर काला
पर सच्चा है साला

(The colour of coal is black
It's raised by mountains
It's black from inside and outside
But it's still real)

His eyes sought out and landed on the face that had made it all possible. He signaled a V and bowed down to him.

Only Samip knew the V stood not for victory but to show the number two; meaning it was not the protégé's victory alone but a coach and student's combined one.

Note: This story was inspired by the theme 'Two' and was first submitted as part of <u>a writing contest for The She Saga's two-year anniversary</u>. It was one of the winning entries.

Our Incomplete Story

"Off to the library again? મુલ્લાહ ની દોડ મસ્જિદ સુધી!"[3] Anant remarked slyly, addressing the quickly darting figure of his classmate and friend.

Shriya rolled her eyes at the comment, choosing to simply answer with a parting wave. After that riveting lecture by professor Joshi, she'd be foolish to not check out books authored by Kanhayalal Munshi.

The minute Joshi sir, their History professor, mentioned that the yesteryear freedom fighter was also a poet and an author, Shriya had let out an audible shriek. The resulting glares from her classmates hadn't pricked her bubble of excitement, as she noted down the names of the books that Joshi sir listed for her perusal.

Once the history lecture ended, Shriya bolted straight out of the classroom.

"There she goes, कमान से निकला तीर[4]."Mansi pointed out, informing Anant; which of course had resulted in Anant teasing the sprinting girl.

Almost panting, Shriya entered the library and shoved her I-card into the librarian's face.

"Slow down, PT USHA. Nobody is stealing our precious books. Not on my watch." Mrs. Khatri chuckled and winked at Shriya, signalling for Shriya to enter and explore the many aisles of the two story library at Saraswati College.

Shriya breathed a sigh of relief, settling down into one of the chairs in the IT room. She quickly typed in Kanhayalal Munshi and jotted down the aisle number and row where she would be able to find the noted author's books.

Taking two steps at a time, she reached the upper floor of the library. There, in the fifth aisle and second last row, perched atop the fourth

---

[3] A Mullah's run is limited to and from the mosque
[4] An arrow shot out of the bow

shelf, she found not one, but two of the books she had on her list from Joshi sir.

"અડધે રસ્તે⁵ and લોપામુદ્ર⁶," Mrs. Khatri's voice had a ting of surprise and admiration as she noted down the titles in her system. She looked at Shriya and added, "We have the English translations for these too. In case you want to read in a language you're more comfortable with."

Shaking her head, Shriya took the books from Mrs. Khatri's hands. Hugging them to her bosom, she said dreamily, "And give up on a story that's been waiting for me to write itself? No way!"

Mrs. Khatri's eyebrows shot up inquiringly, but the younger girl merely shrugged her shoulders and walked out.

Finding her favourite spot empty, she hopped over to the bench beneath the banyan tree. Whistling, she opened the books and took out the notes from each book. She read both the notes again; the reason that had made her pick the Gujarati versions of the books instead of their English translations.

"Oi किताबी कीड़ा⁷. There you are!" A familiar male voice broke Shriya's reverie and she quickly shut the books, stuffing the notes within their pages.

Anant and Mansi walked over and seated themselves next to her on the bench. It was their unified favourite hangout spot and the other two weren't surprised to find Shriya there.

"Gujarati books?" Mansi inquired, taking one of the books from Shriya's lap.

"The English books quota is over or what, that now you're also reading other languages?" Anant butted in, and took the other book.

"Shut up you two. Always with your book jokes. Do I tease you about your cricket and dance passions?" Shriya replied, annoyed, and snatched the books from her friends.

---

[5] name of a book title by Gujarati author Kanhaiyalal Maneklal Munshi, which translates to *Half Way*

[6] name of a book title by Gujarati author Kanhaiyalal Maneklal Munshi, which is the name of maiden named *Lopamudra*

[7] bookworm

"Oho, possessive?" Mansi punched and tickled Shriya's tummy, unrelenting in her pursuit to pull her friend's leg.

"Stop it, Manu!" Shriya shrieked, unable to control her giggling which was a result of Mansi's tickles.

"Okay okay, fine! I'll tell you the reason, please stop." She tried to shove Mansi away, which resulted in both of them toppling off from the bench and onto the ground.

"Oi! What's this? Shri has a secret lover, Manu!"

Anant had managed to get hold of a note from one of the books, while the girls grovelled around before getting their bums back onto the bench.

Shriya covered her face in frustration, not even attempting to stop the drama which was sure to unfold now. Mansi and Anant pored over the contents of the note, oblivious to Shriya's presence for the next few minutes.

"I found a folded note in the library book. There's another one in the other book too. That's the reason I took the Gujarati versions instead of English."

"And, what do you intend to do with them?" Mansi asked with a knowing look, while Anant took out the other note.

In response, Shriya took out her phone, and tapped a few buttons.

रंग थे, नूर था, जब क़रीब तू था
एक जन्नत सा था ये जहाँ
वक्त की रेत पे कुछ मेरे नाम सा
लिख के छोड़ गया तू कहाँ?
हमारी अधूरी कहानी, हमारी अधूरी कहानी
हमारी अधूरी कहानी, हमारी अधूरी कहानी

(There were colors, there was light,
when you were near me.
This world was like heaven..
on the sand of time, you left
Something like my name written..
Our incomplete story)

As the lyrics of the song reverberated in the surroundings, Shriya answered with a smile, "I'm going to find out the hero and heroine of this अधूरी कहानी,[8] what else!"

"How?" Anant and Mansi asked in unison, wearing equally dumbfounded expressions on their faces.

Shriya took the note from Anant's hand. Turning it over, she showed them the text they had missed out.

"Dear Sanchit,
See you at India Gate on December 28, 2024
Yours forever,
Maushami"

"I'm going to India Gate to meet Sanchit and Maushami."

Shriya answered their unasked question.

"And how are you so sure they'll both be there?"

She reread the words on the front of the note again, a hopeful smile playing on her lips.

वह ख़ुशी ही क्या जिसमे तुम न हो
वह फूल ही क्या जिसकी महक में तुम्हरी खुशबू न हो
वह बारिश ही क्या जहाँ भीगने को संग तुम नहीं[9]

Still humming the song, she read the other note.

होंगी बहुत मोहब्बतें संग जीने मरने की
हसरतें तो हमारी भी बहुत तुमसे मिलने की
लेकिन वह इश्क़ ही क्या जिसमे दूरियां न हो[10]

---

[8] An incomplete story

[9] What is that happiness in which you are not there?
What is the fragrance of the flower in which I cannot get a whiff of you?
What is that rainfall in which we do not get soaked together?

[10] There must be many loves who live and die together
I too, long to be with you
But what is love without a bit of distance?

The song came to an end as Shriya turned the note and pointed it out, indicating it to be her response to Anant's question.

"Dear Maushami,
I can't wait to hold you again in my arms after so long.
India Gate will be as special as our college library for me from December 28, 2024
Always yours,
Sanchit"

Shriya looked away dreamily into the horizon, already anticipating *December 28* . For once, she hoped to be part of a love story, even from afar; not unlike those she had grown up reading.

Note: This story was inspired by the prompt 'I found a folded note in the library book' and was first published as part of Blogchatter Blog Hop.

You're the Reason I Smile and Hum

Plink
Plink
Plink

The steady sound of the water dripping from the roof broke the silence of the 12*12 kholi [11]. The inhabitants of the house were mostly unaffected by the sound.

However, Niyati could not ignore the tippity tap of the droplets. She tossed and turned in frustration, intermittently letting out a sigh or a puff. Generally, she was resigned to the slum life and accepted their humble abode and lifestyle with a smile. Today though, she found even her magic carpet, on which she slept every night; the one that gave wings to her many aspirations and dreams, ineffective. She saw it as the thin mattress it was and not Aladdin's jadui kalin [12] that transported her to a better world.

"What's up with you tonight? Generally you snore through storms and thunder." Niyati's mother, Sudha, asked in hushed tones. Her worry was evident even in the darkness and lowered voice.

"When will things improve for us, Ma? Is this how it will always be?"

Sudha lovingly caressed her daughter's face, her eyes determined and hopeful. Instead of responding to her daughter's query, she began humming a song.

धूप आए तो छाँव तुम लाना
ख़्वाहिशों की बारिशों में
भीग संग जाना
(If there is sun, you get the shade
[as in, if there are troubles, you will free me from tensions]
In the rain of wishes,
Get drenched with me.)

---

[11] cabin, small room or hut

[12] Magical (flying) carpet

A smile slowly spread across Niyati's face and she felt her mood lighten. It was their song after all; the one that gave them strength to get through days when the going got tough.

Niyati reached out for her mother's hand and gave it a reassuring press as she joined the older woman in the humming.

जो मिले उसमें काट लेंगे हम
थोड़ी खुशियाँ, थोड़े आंसू
बांट लेंगे हम

(Whatever we get, we'll manage in that.
Some joys, some tears,
We'll divide between us.

Another voice, a muscular one this time, joined them in a few seconds. Soon the full family, including Niyati's father, little brother, and her grandmother, were all singing with her and Sudha.

The quiet that followed after a few seconds, was unaffected by the drips this time. It did have a companion though; the snores of a girl riding high on her magic carpet.

Note: This story was inspired by the word prompt 'Warmth & Energy' representing the colour orange for the Navratri festival. It was first published as part of #AUNavratriBlogHop hosted by Authoropod and Unicorn.

The Moonlight is Raining

"It's been a month already, babe. How long is this going to take?" Mansi cried out in anguish.

"I'm trying my best, love. What else can I do?" Manav answered, trying to pacify his wife.

He had moved from India to Germany in January. As was the protocol, he was asked to come alone first, while his wife, Mansi, would be able to join him after proper documentation and other formalities.

Understandably, the separation was proving hard on both. More so because they had no clarity on the when and how. Also because being in a new country without any friends and relatives, was proving harder on Manav than he had anticipated. Mansi understood this without Manav having to say, because his calls were getting shorter and wider apart; an obvious attempt to hide his feelings.

The next month, there was finally some movement.

"25th March it is baby!" The two lovebirds looked forward to the day when they'd be able to see and hold each after so long.

"I have something to share with you. But only after we meet." Mansi could hardly contain her eagerness, and Manav his curiosity.

But destiny had other plans.

"This Covid had to come this year only!" Mansi was woebegone.

केडी तेरी नाराज़गी
गाल सुन ले राज़ की
जिस्म ये क्या है
खोखली सीपी
रूह दा मोती है तू
(Why are you upset
Listen to this secret
What is this body
It's just an empty shell
You're a pearl of the soul)

"This will be our song baby. Listen to it whenever you miss me and I'll do the same." Manav consoled, while gulping down his own tears.

As the world was locked within the four walls, for Mansi and Manav, the three months turned to four, five, six, seven, eight and it just kept stretching on and on.

"He kicked today."

"How do you know it's a boy?"

"Ouch! Oh my God. I think it's time."

"Baby, I'm there with you okay? Just remember,

तुझ बिन फागुन में फाग नहीं रे
तुझ बिन जागे भी जाग नहीं रे
तेरे बिना ओ माहिया
दिन दरिया, रैन जज़ीरे लगदे ने
(Without you there is no colour in my spring
Without you I'm not awake even when I am
Without you... O beloved
Days feel like ocean, nights as islands)

Manav spent the next few hours holding the phone to his chest, waiting for an update. The song was the only thing keeping him sane.

"Meet Mannat Mishra. I told you it will be a boy." The good news finally came in.

This time Manav let the tears flow, and didn't stop Mansi's either.

"He looks like you, of course." Mansi rolled her eyes, wiping her stained cheeks, as Manav chuckled and blew flying kisses through the phone.

A month later, the family that had grown from two to three, embraced each other at the Frankfurt airport after nine long months.

अधूरी-अधूरी-अधूरी कहानी
अधूरा अलविदा
यूँही यूँही रैना जाए अधूरे सदा
अधूरी-अधूरी-अधूरी कहानी

अधूरा अलविदा

(Our story is incomplete
Our goodbye is incomplete
I hope it doesn't stay like this
Like an incomplete call
Our story is incomplete
Our goodbye is incomplete)

"Of course you had to pick this song." Mansi punched Manav from the backseat, settling Mannat into the baby seat. Two pairs of eyes smiled at each other in the mirror, a tear rolling down two eyes, this time only of happiness and relief.

Note: This story was inspired by the word prompt 'Emotional Balance' representing the colour royal blue for the Navratri festival. It was first published as part of #AUNavratriBlogHop hosted by Authoropod and Unicorn.

That's What Life is All About

किसी की मुस्कुराहटों पे हो निसार
किसी का दर्द मिल सके तो ले उधार
किसी के वास्ते हो तेरे दिल में प्यार
जीना इसी का नाम है
(*Offer yourself to bring a smile to someone*
Share a shoulder to bear someone's pain
Have love for someone in your heart
That's what life is all about)

Getting up, he stretched out his hand, asking her to join him in the dance.

Within the laughter, the two forgot their immediate worries.

Meghna had first met Arjun as a co-worker in an IT firm, where he was her senior. His presence was such that it was hard for anyone within a 300 meter radius around him, not to take notice. With a smile on his face and a joke coming out of his witty mouth every few minutes, nobody was surprised when he found his calling as a stand-up comedian.

"Megha, will you be the muse to this joker and promise to laugh at all my jokes?" His proposal had left her in splits too, and of course she'd said yes.

Their combined salaries had been enough to rent out an apartment back then to start a life together. But as Arjun's comedy career started demanding more of his time, he had to quit his IT job. With one stable income from Megha, and a somewhat fluctuating income from Arjun, the two were just managing to get by over the past few months.

A recent corporate opportunity had seemed promising and things looked better for a while. But today, even that had fallen through.

"If not this, something else will happen or I'll join the company again." Arjun sighed, sounding defeatist for a bit.

मिटे जो प्यार के लिए वो ज़िन्दगी
जले बहार के लिए वो ज़िन्दगी
किसी को न हो हमें तो ऐतबार
जीना इसी का नाम है

(Life is great when it's sacrificed for love
Life is great when it's sacrificed for joy
I have faith in this even if no one else has
That's what life is all about)

This time it was Megha who sang out the lyrics. Continuing their dance, she said, "When that day arrives, I'll have enough jokes to start a career in stand-up myself. How nice, right? That way one of us will always be a joker."

This time it was Arjun whose guffaw echoed around the house, filling it with hope and optimism again.

Note: This story was inspired by the word prompt 'Unparalleled Optimism' representing the colour yellow for the Navratri festival. It was first published as part of #AUNavratriBlogHop hosted by Authoropod and Unicorn.

Stand By My Side, My Beloved

दिल को मेरे हुआ यकीं
हम पहले भी मिले कहीं
सिलसिला ये सदियों का
कोई आज की बात नहीं
(My heart is confident
That we've met somewhere in the past
This is a story of ages
And not something that was crafted today)

The song's lyrics made Suchi smile as she was ushered into the ward. The doctor on duty helped her get comfortable in the bed. Neither of them could see their faces, but the gentle touch and smile were enough indication for Suchi that the doctor was female.

"Welcome to your home away from home" She paused a bit to consult her board, "Mrs. Shah. I am Dr. Amrita Walia and I will be your on-call physician at Healing Hope Hospital."

Even with the protective suit on, Suchi knew she could rely on Dr. Walia. She nodded her head, because that's all her weak body allowed, and Dr. Walia pressed her shoulder pad for assurance.

"There there. No need to worry. We'll defeat this monster together, I promise." Saying that, Dr. Amrita injected the IV tube and started her off on the fluids right away.

Before she could move away, Suchi reached out & stopped Dr. Walia by holding her palm.

"Yes? Do you need something, Mrs. Shah?" She asked, concernedly.

"Why this song?" Suchi asked, curiously. Her weak voice was laced with hope and inquisitiveness.

"Oh, that's my way of keeping the patients in my ward optimistic. I want them to think about that special person who'd support them no matter what. You know, the one they'd want to get back to, healthy and fit. It's my way of giving them strength to fight this monster and get out of here, healed and better."

Suchi's face lit up with a wide smile.

"Oh now you have to tell me. Is it Mr. Shah you're thinking about?" Dr. Walia asked.

Suchi nodded, looking like a teenager in love for the first time.

> हो चांदनी जब तक रात
> देता है हर कोई साथ
> तुम मगर अंधेरों में
> ना छोड़ना मेरा हाथ
> जब कोई बात बिगड़ जाये...
> *(Everyone stands by your side*
> *Till there's a moonlit night*
> *But you my dear, even in the darkness*
> *please don't leave my hand*
> *Whenever something goes wrong...)*

"I'm sure he's waiting for you back home. Why don't you send him this song to remind him that you're thinking of him and that you'll be back soon?"

Saying that, Amrita moved away, leaving a beaming Suchi, who was furiously typing away on her phone.

--

15 days later

Manish waited outside the ward with bated breath. The last two weeks had been nothing short of hell for him; constantly worrying about his beloved and wondering whether she'd make it back home alright.

A smile spread across his face as he saw her being wheeled out. The protective suit was out, but the mask was still on. So was his. Even from behind their masks, Suchi and Manish's smiles reached each other though.

She was talking animatedly to the doctor on her right, who was in a protective suit. As they reached closer, he could hear snippets of their conversation.

"The song kept me optimistic, doctor. Thank you for your support. I was sure I wouldn't be making it back home."

In a gesture totally uncharacteristic of her, Suchi hugged the doctor as she got off the wheelchair.

The doctor hugged back, and, giving Suchi a gentle push, pointed towards Manish.

"Off you go now. Your humnava[13] awaits."

Suchi blushed, and waving a goodbye to the good doctor, rushed forth into the arms of her beloved, healthy and healed.

Note: This story was inspired by the word prompt 'Support' and was first published as part of Blogaberry CC.

---

[13] companion or partner or life partner or partner in a journey

Oh, Something Strange is Happening

तुम पास आए, यूँ मुस्काराए
तुमने ना जाने क्या सपने दिखाए
अब तो मेरा दिल, जागे ना सोता है
क्या करूँ हाय, कुछ कुछ होता है

(You came close to me, and smiled in such a manner
What dreams have you shown me
That my heart, neither stays awake nor does it sleep
Oh, something strange is happening)

"Why do you keep humming this song, Anjali?"

Anjali looked up at Dr. Singh, surprised.

"Whenever we talk about your past, I've noticed you hum this song before answering my questions."

"I'm not sure, Dr. Singh." Anjali answered, looking ruefully at the photograph in her hand.

"Okay, tell me about this photo then. Was it taken at your engagement?"

At this, a smile lit up Anjali's face.

"Yes, that's Aman being his exuberant self, playing with my very heavy chunni[14]." A sigh involuntarily escaped her lips, as she put the photo aside and gazed out of the window, lost in thought.

"Why did you not get married to him then? I can see you're clearly endeared to him."

Anjali chuckled at that. "I wouldn't be here if I could navigate through my complicated feelings now, would I?"

"Fair point. Let's talk about your best friend Rahul then. Do you still love him?"

---

[14] a long scarf that some South Asian women wear around their head and shoulders.

"I thought I did. But when Aman asked me to choose between him and Rahul, I chose neither of them. All I felt was betrayal and anger."

"And why is that?"

"Because I didn't want to be someone's second choice. Rahul never looked at me that way when Tina was around. It was a bit too convenient to his liking. What are me and Tina to him? Just beautiful women to hang on to his arm as candies? Or to bear him babies and take care of them? And the whole, '*we only live once, love once and get married once*' was such a load of crap. Again changed his own philosophy as per his convenience!"

"I see. And?" Dr. Singh probed.

Anjali smiled sadly. Not for the first time, she felt that the counsellor's many accolades weren't for nothing. He somehow always knew things went deeper and that she wasn't revealing the whole picture.

"And I didn't want to do the same thing to Aman as Rahul was doing to me. Clearly I had a lot of baggage to get rid of."

"Acknowledging you need help is the first step. Well done, Anjali."

जान-ए-वफ़ा हो के बेक़रार
बरसों किया मैंने इंतज़ार
पर कभी तूने नहीं ये तब कहा
जो अब कहाँ
दिल बेबसी में चुपके से रोता है
क्या करूँ हाय
कुछ कुछ होता है...

(I had faith in you, but still I was restless
I waited for you for years
But still you never
Said anything then
What you said now
My heart in a helpless state
Cries hidingly

What do I do
Oh, something strange is happening)

6 months later.

Aman couldn't help recalling the song that had changed the course of his life.

He looked at her making his way toward him, her head held up, her shoulders straight; the body language clearly indicating a change in her attitude.

"Thanks for doing this." The two spoke out at the same time, and chuckled, as Anjali took her seat opposite him.

"I wasn't expecting you to want to meet me after..." Aman began.

"And I didn't expect you to say yes after doing what I did."

A few minutes of silence followed, where Anjali looked absently at the menu and Aman observed her, absorbing the features and her movements; the very things that had made him fall for her in the first place.

"You know I can't say no to you Anj." Aman remarked, still not taking his eyes off her.

To his pleasant surprise, Anjali blushed.

This is a first! Aman found himself doing a mental happy dance.

"Aman, I'm still under therapy. But I've decided to give this, *us*, a chance." Anjali revealed. The hesitance in her tone, not missing Aman's ears.

He reached out for her hand. In another surprising feat, she let him.
Who is this new person? Aman mused, taking her palm in his and gently stroking it, then gave it a reassuring press.

"Let's start with friendship first then. After all, love is friendship. Right?"

The reaction was immediate. Anjali snatched her hand out from Aman's grip and threw the menu at his face.

As she stuck her tongue out, Aman couldn't help laughing heartily. More so, out of relief, than anything else.

This time, however, the joke wasn't on him, or their relationship, at least.

Note: This story was inspired by the prompt 'Your favourite fictional characters falling in love' and was first published as part of Blogchatter Blog Hop. It was a featured story under CauseAChatter for its positive message around mental health. It helped Manali receive a badge and a certificate.

The World's Slogan, Stay Vigilant

ये वक्त के कभी गुलाम नहीं
इन्हें किसी बात का ध्यान नहीं

(He is not a slave of time
He has no clue about anything)

"Mom, really?"

"Yes, c'mon get up. Now! I'll keep playing the song till you're out of bed."

I groaned and kicked the quilt off, stomping my feet on the ground as I got up.

"Oh, very subtle. But I'm also your mother, remember?" She walked up to me and landed a whack on the back of my head.

If there was any drowsiness, the remnants of it were now gone. I rubbed the spot where she'd marked me with her love, and dragged my feet to the bathroom.

"Karara jawab milega" [15] I shouted, blew a raspberry and shut the door on her face. You know, before my mother could react or worse, land me another whack.

"Oh, the sheer obstinance! I can't believe I birthed two polar opposite offspring. I'm pretty sure the nurse made a mistake and I was handed the wrong baby."

In case this scene seems familiar, you have my deepest sympathies; we're in the same boat bro, congratulations! And in the off chance that you haven't figured it out yet, I'm the younger **we've probably adopted you** child in an Indian household. My family thinks that because my elder brother is a compulsive over-achiever, I'm compelled to follow in his footsteps or rather his *walk of fame*.

Flash news. It's a big NO, because :

---

[15] Refers to a dialogue from the Hindi movie *Rajneeti* which loosely means *You'll get the answer/ response you deserve*

a. I don't want to, and

B. I have zero motivation to walk even on the sidewalk next to said *walk of fame.*

As the morning went by, I took my own sweet time getting fresh. I then took a leisurely shower before walking out to join the rest of the family for breakfast. I rolled my eyes at the sight of Mayank, my elder brother. As expected, he had his head hanging over an open coursebook in front of him.

Curbing my urge to hit him on the head, I casually took a seat next to him. I whistled and grabbed a banana from the fruit basket and hummed the song which was stuck in my head, courtesy my mother.

क्यों दुनिया का नारा, जमे रहो
क्यों मंज़िल का इशारा, जमे रहो
(Why is the world's slogan ... stay vigilant
Why does our goal beckon ... stay vigilant)

Three sets of scowling faces turned towards me in unison.

"Are you prepared for the examination?" Came the predictable question from my father.

"Of course!" I answered defiantly and went back to my banana.

He turned skeptically towards my mother and the two of them shrugged their shoulders. Great, pretend as if I don't exist. This was their coping mechanism, always.

Honk! Honk!

"C'mon, time to go." Mayank and my mother jumped off their chairs on cue.

The sound indicated the arrival of our school bus. I grabbed a toast and stuffed it in my mouth. I was still hungry and made to grab another banana.

"If only you had woken up a bit early..." My mother grabbed my other hand, resulting in the banana falling from my grip. She snatched my bag which was lying on the table, dragging me behind Mayank, who was already out of the house.

Mayank was getting on to the bus and waved to mom, who blew him a flying kiss.

"All the best, dear."

Then, turning towards me, her endearing expressions changing to a scowl in nanoseconds, she said, "And you..."

"I know, I know. *You better write what you know, Manav. And don't make a fool of yourself.*" I hopped onto the bus and waved to her. I could see a reluctant smile forming on the corner of her lips as she blew a flying kiss to me as well.

"All the best, dear."

The bus turned a corner and soon our mother was out of sight. As per the norm, Mayank took a seat on the last row of the bus. I moved down the aisle, noticing his head bowed down, probably glued inside the coursebook.

I sat a few rows ahead of him, because who wants that kind of negativity in life. Ugh!

Now, before we move ahead with what's happening, let me introduce myself and my nemesis.

Mayank and Manav Ahuja; two siblings who could not be more different from one another. That's what we were known as, throughout Sacred Heart High School, where both of us were currently studying. Him in class XII and myself in class X. Mayank was, as most would say, the teacher's pet and an ideal student. Me, on the other hand, let's just say, I am as far away from ideal as any ICC Trophy is from the Men's Indian Cricket Team currently. That's to say, I have the goods, but I just don't want to use them. See what I mean?

My major concern is, what's the point? Mayank has already done it, so why bother? Anyway, coming back to today, we're both appearing for our board exam prelims. Mayank has his Chemistry paper today and I have English.

If there's one subject I'm good at, it's this. Which explains my chilled out attitude. A little disclaimer here though: this is me almost everyday.

The bus screeched to a halt as I pondered over what topics might show up in today's essay and creative writing section. Excited at the prospect,

I walked out. I was about to walk into my allotted classroom when Mayank called out, "Manav wait!" He ran up to me and handed over a couple of pens and pencils.

"In case you run out of ink. If only you learn to carry a few extra ones yourself. Anyway, all the best." He ruffled my hair and for a change I wasn't irritated. Of course he was right. I had brought only one pen, duh! Because I'm not a nerd, I wanted to justify out loud, but held back my retort.

"Thanks and all the best to you too." I thumped him as he waved dismissively. Then he turned and ran towards his classroom without a backward glance.

Soon the bell rang. I walked into the classroom and took my seat. Once all the students had settled down, we were handed the supplementary and question papers.

Another bell rang indicating we could start answering.

Write up to 500 words on one of the following:
1. When I was caught in the rain without an umbrella
2. If only I had not left it for the last moment...
3. India through my eyes

My stomach grumbled, making me realize I hadn't had a proper breakfast.

"If only you had woken up a bit early..."
"If only you learn to carry a few extra ones yourself..."

I took out my pen, opened the supplement and began writing.

यहाँ अलग अंदाज़ है
जैसे छिड़ता कोई साज़ है
हर काम को टाला करते हैं
ये सपने पाला करते हैं

(Here the style is totally different
As if someone is playing a tune
He procrastinates everything
He has a lot of dreams)

I hummed as I scribbled down my thoughts, chuckling at my own dry humor.

10 years later

"So, Mr. Manav. When was the first time you realized you wanted to be an author?"

This was a new one. I turned toward the front row in the audience and saw my parents seated next to Mayank. They held a united front in the expressions department again. This time though, it was pride rather than exasperation.

"It's a funny story actually. I was appearing for my Class X prelims..."

Note: This story was inspired by the prompt 'If only I had not left it for the last moment…' and was first published as part of Blogchatter Blog Hop.

You're the Sunshine

"Nobody should be surprised with this one." The presenter took a suspenseful pause for a few seconds. Then declared in a booming voice. "The Best Startup Founder of the Year Award goes to Vikas Purohit."

A tumultuous applause broke out in the hall as Vikas walked up to receive the award. He acknowledged his team and thanked the organizers, quickly getting off the stage. The many empty seats adjacent to his, were pricking his bubble of fulfillment and he just wanted to get done with the event.

"Congratulations"
"Wonderful. Sorry I couldn't make it"
"Keep it up. Wish I was there."
The congratulatory messages filled up his WhatsApp and Facebook messenger, as soon as he shared a photo update with the award.

He scoffed, finally pleased with some validation which was a much-needed ego boost. Despite wanting to stay for the after-party and dinner, he had left right after receiving his award and was now already enroute home.

Home?

He realized that his luxurious 4 BHK apartment was merely a house these days.

"Enjoy your wealth and congratulations on all the luxuries!" Nita had said, walking out on him and their relationship almost a year ago. High on his recent successes and the abundance of income which was all new to his lower-middle class upbringing, Vikas had been happy to let her go.

"Go back to where you came from, you twat. That's where you deserve to be. I'll find someone to match my status."

Most women he met after that were only interested in their two minutes of fame with him by their side. They left once their purpose of money and fame was met with. The few who had stayed on, he himself had got bored of after a few dates.

क्यूँ इस कदर हैरान तू
मौसम का है मेहमान तू
ओ दुनिया सजी तेरे लिए
खुद को ज़रा पहचान तू

(Why are you surprised like this
You're a guest to the seasons
The world is decorated for you
Try to recognize yourself)

Standing at the nearby pavement, a young boy was singing the song to a girl, probably trying to motivate her.

"But I'm scared bhaiya[16]."

"I'm right next to you, holding your hand. Come."

Still fearful, the girl held her brother's hand tightly and together they crossed the road, which was bustling with people and moving cars.

Vikas was taken back in time as a feeling of Deja vu overtook him. He was once the boy, and he had sung this very song to a girl scared of the big bad world out there.

"Stop the car." Vikas instructed his driver and got out. He sprinted towards the two kids, quickly catching up with them.

"Wait, hey!"

The boy pushed his sister behind himself, hiding her from view. His challenging stance was at once adorable and laughable.

"Don't worry. I just wanted to ask you, who taught you that song?"

"My teacher, Nita ma'am. She says I should remember my potential through this song."

Vikas hugged the boy impulsively. His gloominess dissipating, he asked the confused boy, "At which school does Nita ma'am teach?"

---

[16] Hindi word for brother

The next day, Vikas found himself at the office of Shree Vidyamandir School.

"But we won't be able to pay you much sir."

"I don't want any money. Just a chance to teach these children."

The principal was dumbstruck. Before he could respond, the well-dressed young man in front of him extended his hand towards him, a cheque outstretched in it.

"In fact, I would like to give something to the institute."

तुझ में अगर प्यास है
बारिश का घर भी पास है
हो... रोके तुझे कोई क्यों भला
संग संग तेरे आकाश है

(If you're thirsty
The house of rain is close by
Why would someone stop you
When the sky is with you)

A chorus singing broke out from a nearby class.
Vikas smiled, feeling complete.
Finally, he had found his true opulence.

Note: This story was inspired by the word prompt 'Opulence' representing the colour purple for the Navratri festival. It was first published as part of #AUNavratriBlogHop hosted by Authoropod and Unicorn.

With Dreams in My Eyes, I've Left From Home

मंज़िल नयी है
अंजना है कारवां
चलना अकेले है यहाँ
तन्हां दिल.. तन्हां सफ़र
ढूंढे तुझे फिर क्यूँ नज़र
(The destination is new
And the caravan is unknown
I have to walk all alone
My heart is lonely... so is this journey
Then why do my eyes keep searching for you)

Shriya felt a gentle tap on her hand. Hastily she wiped the tears as her eyes jerked open. It took her a few seconds to find her bearings while looking around. That's when her sight fell on the figure standing in front of her bus seat.

The crow's feet, and twinkling eyes, were a straight contrast to her frail figure.

"Is this seat taken, my dear?" She asked Shriya, pointing at the adjacent seat. Her soft voice had such a melodious tinge that Shriya found herself wondering how the woman must've sounded in her youthful days.

Shriya shook her head and immediately looked out the window. She then plugged her earplugs back in, clearly indicating she wanted no further interaction. The slight chuckle from her now co-passenger's mouth didn't miss her though. Soon, however, all worldly sounds were drowned out as the lyrics of the song washed over her once again.

दिलकश नज़ारे देखे
झिलमिल सितारे देखे
आँखों में फिर भी तेरा चेहरा है जवां
कितनी बरसातें आई कितनी सौगातें लाई

कानों में फिर भी गूंजे तेरी ही सदा..
(I've seen amazing sceneries
I've seen glittering stars
But your face is still fresh in my eyes
So many monsoons have passed
They brought along with them so many gifts
But still your calls echo in my ears)

In a few seconds, her reverie was broken, one more time with a tap on her left palm. She sighed and gulped down her irritation. *Mustn't forget my manners*, she reminded herself as she opened her eyes and turned to look at her co-passenger.

Her smile was one of concern, which had Shriya's displeasure go down a notch further. Reluctantly, she removed the earplugs, because it was clear the woman wanted to engage in a conversation. She'd expectantly continued to gaze at Shriya's face, her eyes oscillating between Shriya's ears and the headphones dangling on to her chest.

"I'm sorry for being intrusive. Such things come with old age, you see. And we can be forgiven for it too because of the same reason." She chuckled and paused. Seeing no reaction forthcoming from Shriya, she continued. "May I ask which song you're listening to, dear?"

Shriya was slightly surprised, as she'd expected the woman to inquire about her gloomy mood. A bit relieved, she gave a small smile, and offered one of her earphones to the woman. She took it, her enthusiasm matching that of a child being offered free candy. That made Shriya chuckle, suddenly alleviating her mood.

मिट्टी की खुशबू आए
पलकों पे आंसू लाए
पलकों पे रह जायेगा यादों का जहाँ
मंज़िल नयी है अंजना है कारवां
चलना अकेले है यहाँ
तन्हां दिल.. तन्हां सफ़र
ढूंढे तुझे फिर क्यूँ नज़र
(I can smell the fragrance of my home turf
It's bringing tears to my eyes

A universe of memories shall remain on my eyelids
The destination is new
And the caravan is unknown
I have to walk all alone over here
My heart is lonely... so is this journey
Then why do my eyes keep searching for you)

The two women listened to the song together now. The younger one, with her eyes closed in deep contemplation; while the older one, feet tapping and with a smile on her face.

"My name is Sadhna, by the way. And yours?" The older woman asked when the song only had music playing and there were no lyrics.

"I'm Shriya."

Sadhna nodded, the smile on her face had a serene quality; as if knowing Shriya's name told her everything she wanted to understand about the young girl.

After a few minutes, the woman removed her earplug and handed it back to Shriya. She collected her stuff and made to get up, while holding the rod of the seat in front.

She turned to Shriya and said, "It gets better, don't worry." Then she removed something from her bag and put it in Shriya's lap.

Before Shriya could react, respond or understand anything, Sadhna was out of the seat and had disembarked from the bus. Once the bus started moving, Shriya looked out the window. And of course, Sadhna stood there, waving goodbye and shouting, "That's a good combo to have. It makes life easier."

Shriya nodded and waved back, albeit a bit confused, till Sadhna was a mere speck in her vision. Plugging both her earplugs in again, Shriya looked at the gift heaped by Sadhna on her lap.

Iona Iverson's Rules for Commuting by **Clare Pooley.**

Shriya wondered for a few seconds about the how, when and why of it all. Smiling and shaking her head, she opened the book, soon getting engrossed in the world within its pages.

The young girl forgot all about her gloom, and how much she missed her family and home. The smile on her face grew wider with each turning page.

Only when she was about to get down herself and had to close the book did she realize; the combination of music and books was indeed a good one to have, as the old woman's wisdom had envisaged

Note: This story was inspired by the prompt 'On the bus ride home, I met an old lady' and was first published as part of Blogchatter Blog Hop.

New Colours in Every Moment

आगे आगे रास्ता
जो चलता जाता है
सारा सारा ही समां
झूमता गाता है
कोई गीत सुनाता है
(The road ahead
Keeps moving forward
The entire ambiance
Dances and sings
It serenades a song)

"Hey, is that the song you picked for us this festive season, uncle?" Lily inquired.

Aryan smiled evasively before responding to his niece. "That's not how it works, Lil. You will receive your answer with your gift tomorrow morning."

"What if I let you in on a secret?" Lily winked and leaned in towards her uncle. Curious, Aryan complied. After all, he still wanted to hold on to his *Cool Uncle* status even if the kids of the family were catching up in age.

"Mom's recipe of this year is great-grandma's walnut fudge." Lily whispered and then made a notion, sealing her lips.

Teenagers! Aryan muttered to himself, gulping down his chuckle. Although excited at the prospect of finally learning the secret recipe that their grandmother had passed on to her favorite grandchild, he didn't want to let go of this chance to tease Lily.

"Thanks Lil, but I'm still not telling you my song. And I did notice you didn't reveal your secret and chose to give away your mom's. So your request is invalid." He leaned back, enjoying the conflicting emotions on his thirteen-year-old niece's face. Huffing, she stood up and walked away in defiance.

"Hey, Lil. Whatever my choice turns out to be. These lines are for you!" Aryan called after her retreating figure and got back to the keyboard, continuing the song.

नया नया है जोश नए सपने है
यह आसमान ज़मीन सारे अपने है
आओ न इन राहों में

(Renewed enthusiasm and new dreams
The sky and the earth are ours
Come walk on these paths)

Lily turned and blew him a raspberry before walking off into the kitchen.

"Don't mind her. I'm excited to know your pick. Tell me uncle, who started this ritual?" Vicky asked. Aryan turned to his fifteen-year-old nephew, who had just walked into the hall from his bedroom.

"Oh, that credit goes to your great-grandfather and our granddad, Sebastian Mathews." Sophia walked from the kitchen carrying some tissues and a couple of bowls of snacks. "Although I'm sure your uncle Aryan would've lied and taken the credit if I hadn't walked in." She gave her little brother a pointed look.

"I do deserve some credit, Soph. You can't deny that." Aryan said gruffly.

"Oooh how? I want to know this one." Lily said, walking into the hall again, as she and Vicky took seats on the sofa. The two looked at their mother and uncle excitedly, their heads bouncing from one to the other.

"Well, yes, Aryan does deserve some credit. We were about your age and he cribbed one Christmas about receiving such predictable gifts from family and friends. He threw a proper tantrum and even tossed away some of the gifts across the room in agitation."

"In my defense, I received three different train sets. Bringing the total from previous Christmases to ten! At this rate, I could have started my private railway line from our house to every relative's place by next Christmas."

Both Lily and Vicky burst into unanimous laughter, taking a few minutes to get back their bearings.

"You had a thing for toy trains, which given your profession as a railway engineer now, isn't all that horrible. Don't go blaming them for your predictable preferences." Sophia relented, rolling her eyes at her kids and her brother successively. She settled down on the sofa between Lily and Vicky, facing Aryan who was still seated at the keyboard ottoman.

"They could have given me musical gifts, seeing how I was already talking about becoming a singer/musician too. Anyway, so grandpa Sebastian asked me what I would have liked to receive instead and I said a guitar or Casio would've been nice."

"That's when he suggested we could all give two gifts to everyone. One main gift which could either be related to the receiver's profession/study or their hobby, and the other would be a list of recommendations related to the gift giver's profession or hobby For instance a new dish, your favorite reads of the year, movie recommendations, et al. The list has to be accompanied with a gift card using which they can experience or purchase the most recommended item on the list. This would help others decide on the following year's gifts too."

"That is such a cool idea! No wonder great grandpa's gifts were always my favorites." Vicky said.

"Mine too." Lily consented.

"That's why mine is generally song recommendations with a special ***Song of the Year*** list." Aryan revealed.

"And mine is favorite dishes of the year with a ***Recipe of the Year*** list." Sophia nodded and chimed in.

"When dad joined the family, it was favorite reads of the year with a ***Book of the Year*** list?" Lily asked, curious to know more.

Sophia nodded as two more people joined them; a man and a woman, one walking in from the kitchen and the other, from the study.

Before they settled down around the others, Vicky turned to the woman, continuing the discussion, "What's your list of the year going to be, aunt Jasmine?"

She chuckled looking towards her husband, Aryan, before answering, "It was a bit taxing really, first zeroing in on a particular list and then shortlisting my choices to be put in the list. You'll see it tomorrow, love. Have patience." She hugged Vicky, ruffling his hair and steering away from the revelation.

"So this year we'll have two new people joining the ritual, right?" Jasmine rubbed her hands excitedly, happy she wasn't left-out, being the only new addition. Looking at Lily's nervous face, she went over to the freshly in her teens girl.

Taking a seat next to her, she bent down and whispered, "Your guess was right by the way." She winked and looked at Aryan. "That's his song of the year. Also, I'll reveal my list if you reveal yours."

Lily squealed and hugged her aunt, whispering in response.

"Best cafes in the city"

"Best travel destinations"

The two revealed at the same time, hi5ing each other and giggling.

आगे आगे आगे आगे रास्ता
जो चलता जाता है
सारा सारा सारा सारा ही समा
झूमता गाता है
कोई गीत सुनाता है

(The road ahead
Keeps moving forward
The entire ambiance
Dances and sings
It serenades a song)

"I'll bet you your book list for guessing that's Aryan's song of the year," Sophia elbowed her husband, Adam, pointing towards Aryan's singing and keyboard playing figure.

"Hey, no cheating or I'll tell everyone your recipe of the year." Adam elbowed his wife back, a twinkle in his eye.

"And I will tell everyone your book of the year." Vicky butted in, smiling mischievously.

Chuckling, the three then looked on at the virgin pair of Lily and Jasmine with envy and curiosity. Simultaneously, they were all wondering about the eccentricity they'll add to the annual Matthews' Christmas ritual.

Note: This story was inspired by the prompt 'Your favourite christmas ritual' and was first published as part of Blogchatter Blog Hop.

O Mates, I'm a Wanderer

मुसाफ़िर हूँ, यारों
ना घर है, ना ठिकाना
मुझे चलते जाना है
बस चलते जाना

(O mates, I'm a wanderer
I have no house, nor an address
I have to keep moving
I simply need to keep on moving)

Krisha's face lit up on hearing the familiar ringtone.

"Mom, you were right. The train journey is absolutely breath-taking. I'm glad I didn't take a road trip or a flight and did this instead."

"Did you get a window seat? I hope you've taken pictures!"

"Yes to both your questions. You've trained me well, don't worry. Anyway, I'm about to reach Shoghi. Will call you after I reach the campsite."

"Okay, dear. Take care. Enjoy and update me soon. Bye!"

Krisha cut the call and quickly gathered her belongings.

As the train began to slow down, she made her way to the compartment door.

"Ouch!" While getting down, one of her shoes got stuck in a nail that had come off the footboard.

Panicking, she groveled and maneuvered her foot, while muttering in agitation.

After a few seconds of struggle, she finally managed to pull out the shoe before the train's horn blew.

She dragged herself to one of the benches on the station and sat down to assess the damage.

"Damn, I'll have to buy new ones!"

Krisha looked around, and could hardly see more than a handful of people milling about.

"Well, you're no damsel in distress, Miss Krisha." She motivated herself, keeping the dread at bay. Then she opened her backpack, took out the glue she always carried, and managed to fix the shoe, at least temporarily.

"Let's see where we can buy new ones now!" She cheered herself up and walked out of the railway station.

मुसाफ़िर हूँ, यारों
ना घर है, ना ठिकाना
मुझे चलते जाना है
बस चलते जाना

((O mates, I'm a wanderer
I have no house, nor an address
I have to keep moving
I simply need to keep on moving)

Krisha's somber mood turned hopeful as the lyrics of her mother's favorite song reached her ears.

"What a lovely coincidence." She mumbled to herself, making her way towards the shop where the song was playing.

Trinkets & Treasures, Krisha read the board on top of the shop as she entered the cozy space.

"Hello dear. Welcome to Shoghi. How may I help you?" The bespectacled older gentleman behind the counter asked Krisha.

"Is this a retail shop?" Krisha asked after a quick look around the items displayed in the window and racks. It was an odd mix of clothes, scarves, books and old records.

"You can say that, dear." The gentleman replied, a twinkle in his eyes. "Are you looking for something specific? I'm Anand by the way."

"Hello, I'm Krisha. Do you have trekking shoes?" Krisha asked, with hope and doubt in her voice.

"Ah! Of course. Come around to the back." Anand walked towards an aisle at the back of the shop and Krisha followed.

"Take your pick, dear."

Krisha's eyes almost fell out of her sockets.

"Quite a selection, right?" Anand voiced out her thoughts. "These are shoes that tourists leave behind as gifts or forget in their rooms. In fact most items you see here are like that." Anand said, flourishing his hands around the little shop.

Krisha chose the footwear that fit her best, happy that she'd even managed to get them in her favorite color.

She walked around the shop, ensuring they were comfortable enough. That's when her eyes fell on the woolen top displayed on a bust. Impulsively, she reached out to touch it and felt an inexplicable tug to buy it.

"Ah, good choice that one." Anand interjected. "We recycled it recently from two old sweaters. In fact, I was so reluctant to put it up for sale that I used some of the cloth to stitch myself this scarf." He pointed towards his neck, the twinkle in his voice more pronounced. Then he looked away, a wistful look in his eyes.

"I'll take them both." Krisha declared before her mind made her change the decision. Soon after, Krisha took her leave, but not before Anand made her promise to drop in and say bye before leaving town.

Though it wasn't quite winter yet, the weather was a bit chilly. Krisha reached the campsite and took a hot shower to warm herself after the walk from the store to her temporary lodging.

Once dressed after the bath, she clicked a few quick selfies and sent them to her mother.

"Reached the campsite. Loving this town already." She typed a message and pocketed her phone before getting around to unpacking and preparing for the next day's trek.

मुसाफ़िर हूँ, यारों
ना घर है, ना ठिकाना
मुझे चलते जाना है
बस चलते जाना
(O mates, I'm a wanderer

I have no house, nor an address
I have to keep moving
I simply need to keep on moving)

Smiling, she took out her phone, answering her mother's call and chattering off right away.

"Mom, you won't believe..."

"Krish, where did you get that top?"

"It's gorgeous, isn't it? There's this shop here called **Trinkets & Treasures**. It's a kind of a thrift store."

A few deep breaths, and then, "What's the name of its owner?"

"Anand something. I don't know his last name. Why?" Krisha's curiosity peaked.

Silence.

"You know, he was playing your favorite song. That's what made me step into the shop in the first place." Krisha chuckled and continued.

Ashwina, her mother, chuckled too. Then mumbled, "Of course..." She paused and Krisha was sure she heard a sniffle.

"Mom, what's going on?" Krisha asked, concerned.

"Do you remember my Shimla trip I told you about? Back when I was in college?"

"Umm, hmm..."

"I'm sending you a few photos from that trip. Call me once you've received and seen them." Ashwina hung up before Krisha could respond.

Almost immediately, Krisha's phone buzzed incessantly, indicating a barrage of incoming messages.

She opened her WhatsApp to check out the photos. There were around 7-8 of them. As they downloaded, Krisha felt her disbelief mounting as she viewed them one by one.

For the second time in a few hours, Krisha's eyes popped out in shock.

She scrolled through all the photos, going back in time to when she didn't exist; absorbing the reality and marveling at fate's hand.

मुसाफ़िर हूँ, यारों
ना घर है, ना ठिकाना
मुझे चलते जाना है
बस चलते जाना

(O mates, I'm a wanderer
I have no house, nor an address
I have to keep moving
I simply need to keep on moving)

Krisha's hands shivered as she picked up the call; for once the ringtone didn't quite elevate her mood.

"The man you met..."

"Is he my father?" Krisha asked, determined to rip off the bandage right away; trying her best not to sound aggrieved, and failing miserably.

"Krishu, let me explain," Ashwina sniffed, took a pause, and continued after a few deep breaths. "My letters to him after the trip went unanswered. I didn't know how to find him..." With that she broke down completely.

"Mom, mom, please. I don't blame you. I only wish I'd come here earlier."

The two women cried their hearts out together, shedding relentless tears, some with regrets of the past, some with the anticipation and hope of the future.

Note: This story was inspired by the prompt 'You stumble upon a thrift store in a quiet town and find...' and was first published as part of Blogchatter Blog Hop.

My Shadow Will Follow You
Misty Meadows ~ The Idyllic Staycation

A car pulled up in front of the house. The marquee adjacent to it indicated they'd arrived at the right place.

"Hello, Welcome to Misty Meadows."

An elderly gentleman looked up from his book to check out the new guests. Sneha and Pratik smiled at the young man behind the counter who greeted them.

"Thank you. We have a booking for one night under the name Pratik Sahani." Pratik extended his hand for a shake while providing their reservation details.

"Oh yes, I remember. We spoke about a few of your special requests. We have managed to..."

"Yes yes that's wonderful. Thank you so much." Pratik cut him off, looking flustered. He turned to Sneha and was relieved to see that she had busied herself checking out the books on the elaborate bookshelf in the living room across the makeshift front desk. He couldn't help noticing the curious eyes of the elderly gentleman who was observing Sneha with a warm smile.

"Listen, that entire thing is a surprise for my wife. So let's keep it between us, yeah? Mr...?" Pratik turned back and spoke to the young man.

"I'm Ashwin. The owner and co-manager of Misty Meadows."

Ashwin went on to take down Pratik and Sneha's details in the B&B guest register. As he took off a set of keys from one of the hooks behind him, Pratik looked around and couldn't help admiring the overall rustic look and feel of the house. The dull gray-colored masonry walls made the interior pleasant, bordering on chilly. The furniture, right from the rocking chair seating the elderly gentleman to the coffee table in the living room, seemed bespoke. It was either all DIY or Ashwin was uber rich to be able to afford it, because Pratik hadn't seen such designs and finishing on the furniture in his lifetime. Thanks to

Sneha's insistence of *'We have to see and feel the furniture we're buying. I'm not getting this stuff online'* while furnishing their new house, he had his fair share of experience and expertise in the area.

"Here are the keys to your room, sir." Ashwin broke Pratik's admiration streak, handing over the room key.

"That's a good choice. Let me warn you though that it'll keep you up all night." Pratik and Ashwin turned towards the bookcase simultaneously. Sneha, holding a book in her right hand, was looking toward the elderly gentleman with her left hand on her hip, as if asking, "Oh really?"

Pratik suppressed a chuckle as he knew that stance so well. It indicated Sneha was going into battle mode. The elderly gentleman seemed to have caught the whiff too as he chuckled and shrugged his shoulders.

"Well, young lady. Not everyone can handle nighttime adventures in this house. Don't tell me I didn't warn you. " He said and dived back into his own book.

"I'll take my chances." Sneha smiled and replied politely but Pratik knew it actually translated to *Challenge accepted*. Sneha walked back to the counter with the book tucked under her elbow determinedly. Quirking her eyebrows up at Pratik's smile, she asked, "Can we head to the room? I'm tired."

Pratik held up the key to show they were ready.

"It's the room to the right side on the first floor. You won't miss it once you're on the staircase landing." Ashwin smiled as he guided them and wished them a good night.

The room was an easy find as Ashwin had mentioned. Opening the door, Pratik let Sneha go in first. Once inside, she shrieked in delight at the beautiful sight in front of her. There were streamers and fairy lights across the walls and an entire wall with photos of herself and Pratik.

"Happy Anniversary love." Pratik said, embracing his wife from behind.

"Happy five Mr. Sahani." She turned around and hugged him back.

After a candle light dinner set-up for the two inside the room itself, followed by cutting the customized cake, they decided to call it a night. Pratik was snoring within minutes and Sneha lay cuddled inside her duvet with the book she had picked from the shelf earlier.

An hour into it, she had to admit the elderly gentleman had been right. She was gonna be pulling an all-nighter because the book was what bibliophiles like her would call *unputdownable*.

Karen could not believe it. How could he be alive? She had done the deed with her own hands and it hadn't exactly been a walk in the park. She followed the man, picking up her pace before he went out of sight into the next alley.

Sneha turned the page with heightened anticipation. Suddenly she heard a faint sound and looked up. Maybe she had imagined it? She shrugged it off and went back to Karen's discovery.

कभी मुझको याद कर के
जो बहेंगे तेरे आँसू
तो वहीं पे रोक लेंगे उन्हें
आ के मेरे आँसू
तू जिधर का रुख करेगा,
मेरा साया साथ होगा

(If you shed your tears
Remembering me
Then my tears too will come out
To stop them right there
In whichever direction you go,
My shadow will follow you)

There was no mistaking it this time. She jumped up from the bed in alarm. Was someone out there in the hallway? Too chicken to actually open their room and step out, Sneha stuck her ear to the door. She heard the sound of anklets and a chill ran down her spine. Rooted to the spot, Sneha cursed herself for being such a scaredy cat. If not, she'd have confronted the person (or ghost?) on the other side and given them an earful.

तू अगर उदास होगा तो
उदास हूँगी मैं भी
नज़र आऊँ या ना आऊँ,
तेरे पास हूँगी मैं भी
तू कहीं भी जा रहेगा,
मेरा साया साथ होगा

(If you'll be sad
Then I'll be sad as well
I'll be close to you
Whether you see me or not
Wherever you live,
My shadow will follow you)

Sneha glued her ear closer to the door. Wait? This was no Lata Mangeshkar. The voice was definitely melodious, but it didn't seem like the original track. She was about to go on tiptoe and sneak a peek from the eyehole when she felt a hand on her shoulder.

"Argghhhh..." She screamed out in panic.

Confusion mingled with her terror in a few seconds. Was she this loud? Why did her scream sound like that of a man's suddenly?

"What the hell, Sneha?" Pratik's voice reached her ears and she heaved a sigh of relief.

"I heard someone singing outside..." Sneha managed to say in a squeaky voice, still breathing heavily. Was that the sound of her heartbeats? It felt like they would rip through her shirt.

"Man, how many times have I told you not to read thrillers at night? Come on, just go to sleep." Pratik grabbed her hand and literally dragged her to the bed, dumping her in its folds. Without a word, he switched off the night lamp and was off in his dreamland in no time.

"Maybe he's right. It was just a figment of my imagination." Sneha comforted herself in the dark. She forced her eyes shut, and chanting the *Hanuman Chalisa* in her head, slept fitfully through the night.

The sun's rays filtered in through the thin curtains in a few hours.

"Small mercies," Sneha mumbled in her half-awake state, thanking God that it was Summer and that she didn't have to endure the darkness for long.

As soon as both of them were up, she moved at breakneck speed to get ready, pack up and check-out of this creepy place.

At the counter, while Sneha hurried to the bookshelf to return the book she had borrowed, Ashwin asked Pratik, "Happy Anniversary Mr. and Mrs. Sahani. Hope you had a pleasant stay?"

"Yes, we did. Thank you very much."

"So did you like the book?" Sneha jumped out of her skin only to turn around and find the elderly gentleman standing behind her.

"Actually, I couldn't finish it." Sneha replied nervously. Somehow, she couldn't look him in the eye while answering. Noticing her fidgeting with the hem of her shirt, the man went on.

"I hope you weren't disturbed by the nightly adventures of these walls." He laughed. Reaching out behind her, and making Sneha recoil in the process, he grabbed the book she'd just placed on the shelf.

"Consider this a return gift. No one should leave a book unfinished, especially a good one."

Patting her on the shoulder, he turned and settled himself back in his rocking chair. Waving her a goodbye, he was soon immersed in his book.

"Oh no, your wife wasn't imagining that..." Sneha heard Ashwin telling Pratik when she returned to the counter with the book in her hand.

He stopped to give her a smile and continued, "You see, my mother passed away when I was quite young. She was unwell for a long time before the illness took her life. During that time, music and books were the glue that held my parents together."

Ashwin paused to give his father a forlorn look before going on, "The song you heard was in my mother's voice. It was a farewell gift of sorts she left behind for him. He discovered it in his room after her funeral."

Sneha found herself feeling relieved and grief-stricken at the same time.

"He plays it every night?" She couldn't help asking, keeping her eyes trained on the man in the rocking chair. It was hard to believe a fellow bookworm had gone through such a tragic personal experience.

"That's right. Every night since her passing." Ashwin confirmed.

One year later.

The House That Sings by Sneha Sahani

'It seemed that the house whispered at night. Or rather sang its own tunes. As Smriti lay there in her bed, she couldn't help herself from wanting to know more. She needed answers. She had to find out the story behind the voice that was melodious enough to put her to sleep, yet creepy enough to keep her up...."

A tumultuous applause broke through the crowd who had gathered in the café cum bookshop for the launch of Sneha's debut novel.

"May I have my book back please?"

Sneha looked up in surprise.

"Ashok Uncle! I didn't know you were coming." She jumped from the chair and went to hug the man who had inspired the writer in her.

Note: This story was inspired by the prompt 'It seemed that the house whispered at night...' and was first published as part of Blogchatter Blog Hop.

This Intoxicating Evening

"Hey, what's this?"

Sarthak asked his mother, Prerna. He was holding an old, battered-looking, and dust-ridden, square-shaped device.

"Oh my God, I can't believe it's still here." Prerna heaved a deep sigh and held her hand out to her fourteen-year-old son.

Perplexed, Sarthak gave the strange looking machine to her, asking, "But what is it?"

Hugging the device to her chest, Prerna replied with moist eyes, "This is called a boombox. It was the yesteryear version of Spotify from the 70-80s."

Unconvinced, Sarthak looked at the dilapidated box again.

"You mean this is how you listened to music? On this device?" He asked incredulously.

"Mr. I *don't believe you*. Let's get out of here and I'll show you." Prerna ruffled her son's hair, and pulled him out of the room. The mother-son duo was at Prerna's paternal house, clearing it out before putting it up on the market for sale.

"This belonged to your Nanaji. [17]He purchased it with his first earnings in 1972." Prerna continued, plugging the boombox into the power supply.

Shaking her head at her son's dubious expression, she chuckled and checked the cassette tray. Finding it already occupied, she hit the play button.

The room was immediately immersed in the tunes, and lyrics of a Hindi song.

ये शाम मस्तानी
मदहोश किये जाए
मुझे डोर कोई खींचे

---

[17] Hindi word for grandfather

तेरी और लिए जाए

(This evening is lively
It's getting me intoxicated
A string seems seems to be pulling me
Drawing me closer to you)

A smile, unlike any Sarthak had seen in his short life, lit up Prerna's face.

"You know, this was the song that your Nanaji sang for..."

Prerna spoke softly, wiping off a stray tear from the corner of her eyes. She opened her mouth to continue her nostalgia ride but was interrupted when the song suddenly stopped playing. There was a few seconds of static disturbance on the tape, followed by a coughing voice.

"My dear Sarika. I have lost count of the number of times I must have listened to this song. But I do remember that not a single time have I not thought of the way your eyes locked with mine. And the way you blushed when I lip-synced the lyrics, looking your way on a rainy evening."

Prerna let out a gasp, disbelief writ large across her face.

"Isn't that Nanaji?" Sarthak asked, shocked.

She nodded, unable to speak, as the tape went on.

"Remember that evening, Saru? If you don't, I always will. I walked into your father's electronic store. I was merely seeking refuge from the torrential rain. Your melodious voice singing out this song mesmerized me as if seeking me out amidst the thunder and lightning. I knew I was a goner when my eyes fell on you. You were lost in your own world, cleaning the shelves, as the boombox played out Kishore Kumar's voice."

There was a chuckle and a light cough on the tape again. Prerna sniffled and Sarthak rushed forth to give his mother a side hug. The mother and son listened on, fascinated to know what happened next.

"Your father then proudly showed off the boombox to me, trying to convince me to buy it. He said something about it being just delivered fresh from Holland. I gave in, only to get a few more minutes to gaze at you. All the while my eyes followed your movements as you went about humming the song. You didn't acknowledge my presence even once until I myself started humming the lyrics."

There was a few seconds of static on the tape again. A faint voice, as if from far away, could be heard saying, "Karthik ji, come here quickly please."

Sarthak gripped Prerna's hand. His own eyes were a bit moist now. There was no need for either to identify out loud who the other voice belonged to.

A cough, a light chuckle, and the tape went on, "I love it that you need me for such menial tasks. I love it that life is simple, yet so beautiful with you."

There was a shuffle, as if while recording, Karthik was wiping away a tear or two of his own.

"I'm preparing this tape for our special day. I can't believe we're completing 50 years of togetherness. This will be my gift to you. Hope you like it, Saru. Happy Anniversary and thank you for choosing me."

The song came on again.

बात जब मैं करू
मुझे रोक देती है क्यों
तेरी मीठी नज़र
मुझे टोक देती है क्यों
तेरी हया, तेरी शर्म
तेरी कसम मेरे होंठ सिये जाए

(Whenever I talk
Why do you cut me off
Your sweet gaze
Why does it taunt me
Your modesty, your shyness
I swear on you, they seal my lips)

The tape stopped playing and for a few seconds, there was absolute silence. It was as if the walls of the house itself were reliving the moments, lamenting the loss of its owners.

Ruffling Sarthak's hair, Prerna began in a choked voice.

"Your name is a combination of their names you know?"

Sarthak's reply came out in a squeak. His attempt at trying to camouflage his emotional side, quite apparent.

"Yes, Nanu[18] told me how you insisted on it because I was born on their anniversary."

Prerna walked over to the boombox. Hugging it one last time, she put it on top of the ever-towering pile of things to be discarded.

She dusted hands on her hips, and let out a sigh, before moving back to the room they had been clearing.

"You coming?" She called out to her son.

Sarthak quickly slipped the boombox into his bag.

"Nanu, you and your Saru will be safe with me. After all, I'm part you and part her. So how can I let go of something that brought you together, right?"

> ये शाम मस्तानी
> मदहोश किये जाए
> मुझे डोर कोई खींचे
> तेरी और लिए जाए
> *(This evening is lively*
> *It's getting me intoxicated*
> *A string seems to be pulling me*
> *Drawing me closer to you)*

He hummed as he went back to join his mother, pondering over the power of music. And how a song and an obsolete device connected three generations.

Note: This story was inspired by the prompt 'A short story inspired by your favourite song' and was first published as part of Blogchatter Blog Hop.

---

[18] Short for Nanaji, meaning, grandfather

Story of My Journey

"But it's risky sir. We strongly recommend keeping her here instead of outpatient care."

"I don't know, Dr. Arora. That's all she talks about these days whenever I visit." Sumit's voice broke and a sniff followed.

Though tired and falling in and out of sleep, Sunita caught bits of the conversation; enough to understand and feel Sumit's agitation.

She wanted to reach out to him but her body didn't allow her.

Damn old age. And damn these medications.

She cursed in her mind, trying to get into a more comfortable position.

However much everyone around her tried to hide it from her, Sunita knew her end was coming. That much she knew her body, if not anything else.

"Promise me, Suni. Only then I'll go in peace." Amit's last words acted as the energy pill she required and Sunita's eyes flew open right away.

"Sumit, dear. Can you come to me please?" She called out in a croaky voice.

She heard shuffling of feet, followed by the creaking sound of the door.

Soon, her son, Sumit, was beside her, holding her hand in the most tender way. His eyes were swollen. Though he had rubbed away the tears, the stains on his cheeks spoke of the anguish he was trying to mask behind the smile.

"Did I ever tell you how your father and I decided on your name?"

Sumit shook his head, pressing her palm gently; encouraging her to go on.

"It was the closest we could agree on the combination of our names- Sunita and Amit. There were others like Nitin, Mitul, Sunit and what not." She chuckled, moving her hand over his face adoringly. With the little strength she had, she pulled his face closer to hers, and planted a kiss on his temple.

"Consider this my last wish, son."

Sumit pressed his lips and wiping away the tears, walked out of the room.

"I kept my promise, Amu." She kept mumbling as Sumit, Dr. Arora and a couple of nurses moved her from the room into the car.

The sight that greeted her in a few hours, was the one she'd been dreaming about for a decade. She reached out her hand and moved it over the plaque on the bench.

Of course, Sumit knew where she'd want to be.

"Amit N. Sanghani," Sunita read out the name and took in the expansive park she'd fought tooth and nail to build.

She closed her eyes, taking a deep breath. A gust of air blew over her face, moving away her hair, and caressing her cheeks.

"I'm here, Amit."

She heard the notes of dhol and shehnai in the distance. She saw the place as it was on that day, 50 years ago; the day they became Mr. and Mrs.

ओ सफ़रनामा
सवालों का सफ़रनामा
शुरू तुमसे, ख़तम तुमपे सफ़रनामा

*(O, the story of my journey
A travel narrative of questions,
It begins from you, ends at you, this narrative)*

How apt! She thought to herself, smiling.

After that everything went blank.

Note: This story was inspired by the word prompt 'Peace' representing the colour white for the Navratri festival. It was first published as part of #AUNavratriBlogHop hosted by Authoropod and Unicorn.

My Footprints are Your Companion

2011

धुंधला जाएँ जो मंज़िलें
इक पल को तू नज़र झुका
*(If the destinations get hazy
Turn your gaze down for a moment)*

"C'mon join me, Aarav."

झुक जाये सर जहाँ वहीं
मिलता है रब का रास्ता
*(Wherever your head bows down
It will lead you to the path to God)*

"Yes, louder this time."

तेरी किस्मत तू बदल दे
रख हिम्मत बस चल दे
तेरा साथी, मेरे कदमों के हैं निशाँ
तू न जाने आस पास हैं खुदा
*(Change your destiny
Be strong and keep moving on
My footprints are your companion
You don't know it, but God is nearby)*

Nilima hugged her son, tears flowing down her cheeks in earnest. For once, she did not even try to hide or wipe them out. Today, she wasn't afraid of how and what she'd say about the reason for such an emotional breakdown. She wanted to cherish this moment as not many such would be coming her way in the short time she had left.

"It's okay, mom. I'm here." Aarav hugged Nilima back tightly, brushing off the tears from her face.

She looked at her tween son curiously, and with a bit of pride, wondering when he'd grown so mature.

"I want you to remember this song and this moment whenever you feel alone or scared. Promise me this, okay?" She held out her pinky finger.

"Yes, mom. I promise."

***

2023

25 severely injured, 5 with minor injuries, but a miraculous 0 deaths in a bus accident on Samruddhi Expressway. Local young boy saves the day

30 passengers were injured after a bus fell into a roadside waterbody on Thursday night at Buldhana District in Maharashtra on Samruddhi Expressway. The passengers were rescued and taken to a local hospital from where they were discharged after necessary treatment. According to sources, on Thursday night, an air-conditioned bus was moving towards Mumbai from Buldhana along the Samruddhi Expressway. While passing by Nagpur, the bus hit a pole on the expressway and one of its tyres got punctured. Due to the incident, the driver lost control and the bus fell into the water body. While most passengers struggled to stay afloat and many were close to drowning, Aarav Mehta, a 25-year-old, took it upon himself to save the day. He carried each of his co-passengers to safety on his shoulders, swimming back and forth from the lake to the shore, till all 30, including the driver, were on dry land. The local police and medical staff were informed by then, who ensured that all victims were taken to the nearest hospital at the earliest. A statement was released by the authorities in a few hours, ensuring that all passengers were recovering and there were no deaths recorded.

"And now, we have with us the youngest ever recipient of the Bharat Ratna, Mr. Aarav Nilima Mehta. Mr. Mehta, can you tell us what inspired you to stay calm and help your fellow passengers after the bus overturned and fell into the river?"

The camera zoomed in on the young man seated on the sofa. It was a press conference for the recipients of one of the highest civilian awards in India.

Aarav smiled politely and began to answer, "It was my mother."

"Your mother? Was she also traveling with you on the bus?"

Aarav looked upwards and blew a flying kiss into the sky.

"Yes, her footprints are always my companion." He answered, hand on his heart.

A unanimous gasp followed from the interviewer and the spectators. A few sniffs could be heard too.

"But weren't you afraid of losing your own life down in the water?"

"No, I just kept hearing my mother's voice saying रख हिम्मत बस चल दे, तू न जाने आस पास हैं खुदा [19] and that was all I needed."

In the applause that followed, Aarav could feel a familiar voice humming out a song he'd never forget.

Note: This story was inspired by the word prompt 'Infinite Courage' representing the colour red for the Navratri festival. It was first published as part of #AUNavratriBlogHop hosted by Authoropod and Unicorn.

---

[19] Be strong and keep moving on, you don't know it but God is nearby

Come Back Home

13 July 2011

"Hey, Mayank. Are you ready? Let's get this done soon. I'm really tired today."

"Yes, bro. Just give me a second. I'll collect the certificates that we have to hand over."

Samarth nodded and took a seat at the sofa in the foyer. Mayank and he worked as Consultants cum Quality Assurance Technicians at Payal Jewelers. They had joined the store almost together, a little over a year ago. Being from families that had been in the jewelry business for generations, they had similar backstories. Before joining the family business, their fathers had asked them to get an understanding of the industry by training under someone else. For both youngsters, Payal Jewelers had been their first choice because of its goodwill.

"Let's go. Have you been to Mr. Mehta's shop before? It's near Khau Gali. Let's have a couple of pudlas[20] from Mohanbhai before we meet Mr. Mehta." Mayank suggested, as they walked out of the showroom and into the bustling streets of Zaveri Bazar.

क्यूँ देश-बिदेश फिरे मारा
क्यूँ हाल-बेहाल थका हारा
क्यूँ देश-बिदेश फिरे मारा
तू रात बिरात का बंजारा
ओ नादान परिंदे घर आजा

(Why do you roam around countries and foreign lands
Why are you in such a bad state
Why do you roam around countries and foreign lands
You've become a wanderer of nights
O naive bird, come back home)

---

[20] thin pancakes or crepes made most commonly with besan flour (also known as chickpea or gram flour)

Before Samarth could respond, they were interrupted by the ringing of his cell phone. It was the custom tone he had set for his mother.

"Hey, mom. I'll be a little late today. Mayank and I have to drop off some diamond grading certificates at another shop."

"Let Mayank go alone dear. You're needed here. Bhavisha has gone into labour."

A mix of anxiety and exhilaration surged through Samarth.

"I'll be there as soon as possible, mom. See you at the hospital directly. Take care of Bhavu and tell her I'll be with her in half an hour."

Samarth cut off the phone, already bouncing up and down on his toes.

"Go on, man. I'll finish this. Congratulations in advance. Remember if it's a boy, you have to name him after me." Mayank winked and thumped Samarth. At Samarth's hesitation, he merely laughed and gave him a little shove towards the street exit.

"Thanks, man. I'll see you tomorrow." Samarth gave his friend a side hug and sprinted towards the railway station, excited at the prospect of becoming a father.

***

13 July 2021

"Dad, where were you when this happened? Weren't you working at Zaveri Bazaar that year?"

Samarth looked at the newspaper article his son was reading.

10 years since triple blasts left 27 dead in Mumbai, trial yet to commence

The headline brought back repressed memories, alongside the guilt and trauma that had followed. His eyes pooled up with unshed tears.

Sniffling, he answered with a jerky smile, "Let me tell you about a phone call that changed my life, Mayank. It was the day I lost a friend and found you."

कागा कागा रे मोरी इतनी अरज तोसे
चुन चुन खाइयो मांस
अरजिया रे खाइयों ना तू नैना मोरे

> खाइयों ना तू नैना मोहे
> पिया के मिलान की आस
>
> *(Hey lost raven, I have a request for you*
> *Eat my meat selectively*
> *I request you,*
> *Don't gauge out my eyes*
> *Because I yearn to see my beloved)*

Samarth hummed, before beginning the tale.

Note: This story was inspired by the prompt 'A phone call that changed my life' and was first published as part of Blogchatter Blog Hop.

This Beautiful Night, Might Not Come Again

हमको मिली हैं आज, ये घड़ियाँ नसीब से
जी भर के देख लीजिये हमको क़रीब से
*(I was fortunate enough to get these precious moments today
Look at me closely and to your heart's desires, sweetheart)*

As was the norm, I was listening to our cue song, awaiting their arrival. Slowly but steadily, the cosmos around me changed colours. The world had just witnessed another beautiful sunset and was now slowly getting embraced in the clutches of the dark.

My reverie was broken during the next stanza, by a rattling sound.

Who could that be? I wasn't expecting them so soon.

Silence.

I ignored the disturbance and let the magical lyrics engulf me again.

पास आइये कि हम नहीं आएंगे बार-बार
बाहें गले में डाल के हम रो लें ज़ार-ज़ार
*(Come closer, because I will not be able to come to you again & again.
Put your arms around me and let us cry out)*

Tick Tick
Tick Tick

There it was, louder and more insistent this time, followed by a series of footsteps.

Creak

The unmistakable opening of a door.

I stayed rooted to my spot, gripped by a sense of foreboding.

Clomp

Clomp

Two visitors, judging by the gaps between the footsteps.

लग जा गले कि फिर ये हसीं रात हो न हो
शायद फिर इस जनम में मुलाक़ात हो न हो
(*Embrace me, dear, who knows whether or not this beautiful night will ever come again*
In this incarnation, we may or may never meet again)

One of them, a man, continued the song in a voice that didn't quite match the tone or the gender of the actual song. It would be funny otherwise, however, I felt a bile rising up my throat.

Could this be another one?

Thud
Thud

The uncanny familiar sound of the earth being dug up.
Thud
A louder one this time.

Were they burying a body?

"Hurry up, please. Stop singing the song too. Argh! So creepy."

"Shut up! We wouldn't be here if you could keep it in your pants for once."

Two men then.

Scrap
Scrap
Thud
Thud

The sounds grew more rapid. After a few minutes, the thudding stopped and there were only rasping breathing sounds, slowly fading away.

Clomp
Clomp
Creak
Click

Silence.

आँखों से फिर ये प्यार कि बरसात हो न हो
शायद फिर इस जनम में मुलाक़ात हो न हो
(The rain of love in our eyes may or may not happen again.
Maybe we'll meet again in this incarnation, maybe we won't)

Our congregation finally convened.

"We have a new member. Share your story." I began.

"I was at a party, dancing and having fun. Some boys joined us as they knew someone in our group. I don't remember when the party ended or with whom I left. I was in and out of consciousness after that, in some dark place. I could make out the bruises on my body and felt an increasing ache every time I gained consciousness. There were hoots and laughter at some intervals too." She shuddered. I gave her hand a squeeze.

"Maybe hours, days, or weeks later, I woke up in the middle of the night, and I felt a cold hand touching my face. I tried to scream, but my voice wouldn't come out. Then I felt a sharp pain in my neck. And now, here I am."

"Welcome to a better world." The youngest of us, a three-year-old, said.

"Their blood will be next. Justice be served." We promised in unison, raising our chalets and taking a long sip.

Note: This story was inspired by the prompt 'I woke up in the middle of the night, and I felt a cold hand touching my face. I tried to scream, but my voice wouldn't come out. Then I felt a sharp pain in my neck'. It was written as part of the Halloween writing contest hosted by Authoropod. It received a <u>special mention</u> and was published in the <u>January 2024 issue</u> of the magazine.

This Heart Says, Live a Little

मैं हूँ गुमसुम
तू भी ख़ामोश है
सच है समय
का ही सब दोष है
धड़कन धड़कन
इक ग़म रहता है

(I don't have words
And you're silent as well
It's true that
Time is to blame for everything
In every heartbeat
There's a sadness)

Manish sighed as he pushed the door of their two-bedroom apartment, taking out his earplugs in the process.

Another day of going through the routine. And a few more more hours of wondering what went wrong. At least now they'd grown out of blaming each other for it.

After half an hour, Sharda and Manish sat at the table, gulping down their dinner in silence. As was the dictated norm over the past five years, no words were exchanged between the couple. It was a chore, like any other; not unlike their professional duties. In fact, to an observer, it might even look more dull than a client pitch presentation by Manish or conducting a poetry class for young minds by Sharda. They would at least smile there, which was even genuine on most occasions. Here, there were no pretenses either.

This on the other hand... felt strained. Like even a little noise would shatter everything.

The clitter clatter of the spoons on plates was broken by the scraping chairs.

"Good night" said Manish, retiring to his room, not acknowledging or noticing Sharda's responsive, imperceptible nod.

> है ज़िन्दगी माना
> दर्द भरी
> फिर भी इसमें ये
> राहत भी है
>
> *(I agree that life is full of pain*
> *But it still it has moments of relief in it)*

With earplugs back in, Manish set down to complete another routine. After the incident, he'd taken up this habit. It was more out of spite than anything else, as if he were challenging fate.

While matching the numbers on the two tabs, Manish's disbelief grew with each reading. On completion, still dumbstruck, he rechecked at least ten times to ensure he'd read the sequence and all the numbers on the ticket right.

Then, in a daze, he called up the number provided on the ticket.

"Yes, sir. That is the correct number for today's winning lottery. Congratulations. Please visit our website and enter all the details to claim your prize."

For the next quarter of an hour, as if in a trance, Manish filled out the form on the website.

Before retiring to bed for the day, he walked over to the other room. With trepidation, he slowly opened the door. Sharda lay on the bed, turned to the side where he couldn't see her face. Her snoring sounds filled up an otherwise silent room. Manish knew, both the acts were a ploy to avoid conversation; turning the other side and the fake snores.

Unlike other days though, a smile passed his face.

> जी ले ज़रा जी ले ज़रा
> कहता है दिल जी ले ज़रा
> ए हमसफ़र ए हमनवा
> आ पास आ जी ले ज़रा
>
> *(Live a little*
> *This heart says, live a little*
> *My companion, my beloved*
> *Come close to me and live a little)*

He walked back to his room, humming the song as a peaceful sleep, without any nightmares of the accident, overtook him.

Four months later

Sharda climbed up the stairs of the building, her purse and groceries in hand. It had been another uneventful day of lectures and interactions with the students and other professors.

At least it keeps me distracted. And provides some happiness.

She sighed, unlocking the door of their two-bedroom apartment, and entering it with increased dread.

As she placed her purse and groceries on the table, her eyes went to a fancy envelope placed in the center.

She opened it with curiosity, not at all anticipating and completely taken by surprise with what lay inside.

Dear Mrs. Sharda Thakur

Please grace us with your presence at the inauguration of **Shaish Retreat- A Haven for Good Intentions**. *The venue and timing for the event has been mentioned below. PTO for a reference photograph of the institute.*

Mr. Manish Thakur, our founder, requests your company for the auspicious ribbon-cutting ceremony, followed by a Shanti Puja.

We look forward to having you with us.

--

So that explains the sudden cheerful aura and prolonged absences, Sharda thought, putting two and two together.

All along, as she got ready, stepped out of the house, and in the cab, a smile lingered on Sharda's lips.

ग़म के ये बादल
गुज़र जाने दे
अब ज़िन्दगी को
निखार जाने दे
छोड़ दे अब यादों

> के दुःख सहना
> सुन भी ले जो
> दिल का है कहना
>
> *(Let these clouds of sorrow pass by*
> *Let life start blossoming*
> *Stop bearing the pain of memories*
> *Listen to what the heart is saying)*

Sharda listened to the song and a silent tear rolled down her cheek. She wiped it, finally understanding why her husband had been humming these lines in her presence for the past few weeks.

The cab halted outside the huge ornate metal doors, greeting her with a pleasant sight.

"That's a fitting tribute", she said, walking over behind Manish, who stood at the right side of the gate.

In loving memory of Shaish Thakur
A beloved son
A lone warrior

Sharda read out the plaque below the head bust, reaching out for Manish's hand. Giving Manish's hand a little squeeze, she placed her head on his shoulder. Together, the grieving parents walked down the path, towards their healing.

Note: This story was inspired by the prompt 'You just won 1 million at the lottery' and was first published as part of Blogchatter Blog Hop.

I Blindly Tread this Path

मेरा कर्म तू ही जाने
क्या बुरा है क्या भला
तेरे रास्ते पे मैं तो आँख मूँद के चला
तेरे नाम की,
जोत ने सारा हर लिया तमस मेरा

(My karma is bestowed to you
You decide my good and my evil
I blindly tread the path you have chosen for me
Your light ignites my universe
And swallows my darkness)

Arnav rushed into the house, avoiding his father Prakash's eyes, and joined in the evening aarti. Without breaking his monotone, Prakash's eyes flicked over Arnav's figure, giving a disapproving look before turning back to the Shiva idol.

Arnav flinched, fully aware that a tirade awaited him at the other side of the aarti. For now though, he let the sounds of the bells, cymbals and the lyrics of the aarti wash over him. Within just a few seconds, he felt at peace; all his anxiety of the past few hours forgotten.

नमो नमो जी शंकरा
भोलेनाथ शंकरा
जय त्रिलोकनाथ शम्भू
हे शिवाय शंकरा
नमो नमो जी शंकरा
भोलेनाथ शंकरा
रुद्रदेव हे महेश्वरा
रुद्रदेव हे महेश्वरा
रुद्रदेव हे महेश्वरा

(Hail the Greatest God
My beloved kind-hearted Lord
Hail the Creator,

Hail the Originator
Hail the Greatest God
My beloved kind-hearted Lord
The abode of joy
The abode of joy
The abode of joy)

The end notes of the aarti reverberated through their home temple. The bells, cymbals and the claps subsided after a few seconds.

"Har Har Mahadev[21]" Prakash's voice boomed, followed by the others who repeated the chant after him. Three times, as had been the norm, since Arnav could remember. Only the person saying the chant had changed from the past few months.

All the visitors collected the prasad[22] from the thali in Prakash's hand, before bowing down to the deity and then bidding farewell to Prakash with folded hands. Slowly, they trickled out of the house, leaving behind just the father and son.

At last, Arnav walked up to Prakash and took his blessings.

"Baba[23], I got…" Prakash grunted and held up his hand, interrupting Arnav, and indicating that the conversation was to be kept on hold.

After placing the brass lamp and the prasad at the feet of the 20 inch Shiva idol, Prakash touched its feet. Arnav followed suit.

Turning off all the lights in the temple room, they walked out and seated themselves on the sofa. Once settled, Prakash looked inquiringly at Arnav, eyebrows quirked up, and lips pursed.

"Sorry baba, I got late because something came up at work and then…"

---

[21] An incantation/chant that means 'Everyone is Lord Shiva' or "Please take away (destroy) my sorrow and ignorance, O Lord Shiva."
[22] Anything, typically food, that is first offered to a deity or saint and then distributed in His or Her name to their followers or others as a good sign. 'Prasāda' is sometimes translated as gift or grace.
[23] father: used by some South Asians to refer to their fathers or show respect to an older man

"Is it done?" Prakash cut off Arnav's tirade gruffly.

"My work? Yes, of course..." Raised eyebrows, followed by a grunt and sigh from Prakash, made Arnav stop mid sentence; yet again.

Prakash shook his head and turned to look outside the window. The sun had set half an hour ago but the sky was still bright. One could see flocks of birds flying away to their nests amid the orange and purple hues. It was their favorite hour, one where he and Sunita would sit sipping their teas, making plans for which Shiva temple to visit next. This year they were planning the biggest pilgrims of all. Until...

Prakash turned to Arnav, who was looking at him, perplexed.

"I mean the tickets, Arnav."

Arnav hit his forehead with his right palm and stuck his tongue out, muttering, "Aiyo[24]". With a pang, Prakash was reminded of Sunita.

He looks and behaves so much like her. It's painful yet satisfying.

Another involuntary sigh escaped Prakash's mouth as he turned to look at the sky again.

"Yes that too, baba. That's why I was late. A friend called up to say that his family are cancelling and we could get our tickets reserved in their place. So we rushed to the railway station. I didn't want to come home and rely on online booking lest we miss our chance again."

With a broad smile, Arnav took out two pieces of paper from his pocket.

"Here are our tickets for the Chaar Dham Yatra[25]."

Prakash instinctively jumped up in delight, giving his son a tight hug. He kissed him on the forehead and ruffled his hair, wiping away a stray tear from his cheek.

---

[24] (in southern Indian and Sri Lankan English) used to express distress, regret, or grief.

[25] Char Dham means "four abodes or seats of god". It included four pious spots scattered in four directions of India - Dwarka (west), Badrinath (north), Puri (east) and Rameshwaram (south). Yatra (or pilgrimage) in Hindu religion is considered as one of the ways of attaining Moksha.

He then walked into the temple room again, rang the bell and bowed his head in reverence.

"Har Har Mahadev" he boomed and Arnav repeated after him.

Before Prakash came out, Arnav rushed to the huge portrait in the living room.

He bowed and touched his head to the frame. Then folding his hands, he addressed the woman in the picture, "I wish you could come with us too, aai[26]."

Prakash joined him, and throwing his hand around Arnav's shoulders, he said, "I wish that too, son. After all, it was her life long dream. I just wish I hadn't waited so long to fulfill it."

Both father and son wiped away each other's tears, crying in memory of the woman who had brought the sublimity of Mahadev into their lives.

Note: This story was inspired by the word prompt 'Bells' and was first published as part of Blogaberry CC.

---

[26] Mother-used by some South Asians to refer to their mom

P. S.: Before reading ahead, here's your reminder to go back to the poem in the <u>prologue</u>.
Psst! Don't forget my promise.

Note: In case it didn't come across as I intended, here's what the poem represents. Each stanza in the poem is meant as a summarisation of a story from the collection. The stanzas are chronological, meaning, they represent each story in the order that it appears in the book

Playlist

Each story title in this collection is an English translation of a Hindi song. Most stories have the lyrics of the song imbibed into the plot as well. Provided below is a list of all the songs, in order of the song/story title appearances in the book.

Song	(Corresponding) Story Title
Rim Jhim Gire Sawan	The Rain Falls Pitter Patter
Khwaabon Ke Parindey	In the Free Sky, Let My Dreams Fly Like the Birds
Ye Mausam Ka Jadoo Hai Mitwa	It's the Magic of the Season
Ye Moh Moh Ke Dhaage	These Threads of Love, Entwined with Your Fingers
Kabhi Neem Neem	Sometimes Bitter, Sometimes Sweet
Abhi Na Jao Chhod Kar	Don't go Just Yet
Atrangi Yaari	My Companion of this Crazy World
Aahatein	It Didn't Happen to Me, Why Did it Happen to You Then?
Mann Ki Lagan	My Heart Has Started to Love You
Zinda	The Coal is Black and Raised by Mountains
Humari Adhuri Kahaani	Our Incomplete Story

Muskuraane Ki Wajah	You're the Reason I Smile and Hum
Chandaniyaan	The Moonlight is Raining
Kisi Ki Muskurahaton Se Ho Nisar	That's What Life is All About
Jab Koi Baat Bigad Jaaye	Stand by My Side, My Beloved
Kuch Kuch Hota Hai	Oh, Something Strange is Happening
Jame raho	The World's Slogan, Stay Vigilant
Kholo Kholo	You're the Sunshine
Tanha Dil	With Dreams in My Eyes, I've Left from Home
In Raahon Mein	New Colours in Every Moment
Musafir Hoon Yaaron	O Mates, I'm a Wanderer
Mera Saaya	My Shadow Will Follow You
Ye Shaam Mastani	This Intoxicating Evening
Safarnama	Story of My Journey
Aas Paas Khuda	My Footprints are Your Companion
Naadan Parinde	Come Back Home
Lag Jaa Gale	This Beautiful Night, Might Not Come Again
Jee Le Zara	This Heart Says, Live a Little

| Namo Namo | I Blindly Tread This Path |

Listen to the songs on YouTube, Spotify and Amazon Music

Other Books by This Author

Love (Try) Angle (Love Trials I)

Ayesha has just moved to the 'City of Dreams' with her parents. She befriends the charming Viren, who helps her find her footing in Mumbai. Though she is slowly adjusting to her new life, what Ayesha is most excited about is pursuing B.A. (Hons.) Political Science from a reputed college. Things don't go as smoothly as she had thought though. Because Abhi, her senior, seems hell-bent on making her life on the campus difficult from day one. Just when things seem settled, Viren joins the college as an Ad-Hoc lecturer. Is there more to Ayesha's friendship with Viren, and her frenemity with Abhi? It seems there's a love triangle blooming around the corner or will it be a Love (Try) Angle? Because Ayesha is not sure if it's love at all.

Love & (Mellow) Drama - Love Trials II

Gayatri Kulkarni: A Gen-Z girl who has always lived under the shadow of her elder brother Sharad; so much so that she even chose her degree and college following in his footsteps. Although she doesn't regret it, she wishes her parents would understand her dream to pursue her one true passion - DANCE.
Varun Agarwal: A millennial who believes there are no shortcuts in life. He has learned the hard way that being born into a wealthy family comes with more cons than the world would ever understand.
She belongs to a Maharashtrian middle-class family from the suburbs. He hails from an affluent family in South Bombay. The only common point between them - being Mumbaikars. How do their paths cross in this city of dreams? Gayatri believes it's because of Abhi Agarwal, Varun's younger brother, who also happens to be her brother's batchmate and close friend. But Varun has harboured a crush on her long before they exchanged hellos and phone numbers.
Their story is a meeting of two generations and families, who are poles

apart. Is there drama involved? Gayatri is often called a drama queen by those who know her. But after Varun's entry into her life, she's transformed from Miss Melodrama to Miss Mellowed Drama. Find out all about that transition in this much-awaited spin-off from Manali Desai's debut novel, ***Love (Try) Angle, Love & (Mellow) Drama (Love Trials-II)***

<u>Night in Shining Armour</u>

This little book brings forth a collection of poems, each centered on and around the theme of nightly experiences and encounters. Right from dinner dates to bonfires and stargazing, almost every activity that happens after sundown is covered herein, in poetic verse. Divided into two sections- Facets and Pursuits; the poems in Facets are a night lover's ode to the elements of the dark, and those in Pursuits, talk about nighttime occurrences and indulgences. Striking a chord with nocturnal (human) beings and selenophiles, the lines herein are assured to evoke emotions of longing. No human, irrespective of their age is deprived of the pleasures (or pains) that the dark hour brings in. The poems, describing moments of what happens after sundown will make the readers romanticize the darkness or have bittersweet moments flash through their minds, helping them relive and reminisce long forgotten or buried memories.

Mindful Musings & Peaceful Ponderings

Anxious

Conflicted

Nervous

Confused

Safe

Complete

Jubilant

Confident

Do these sound familiar? You may not have experienced these *feelings* lately or maybe not at all. But if you have, you aren't alone. The 50 poems in this book are a reflection of you, me, and all of us. They are the mindful musings and peaceful ponderings of human experiences that make us smile, laugh, cry, and wonder with emotions, that unite us all.

Under the Mistletoe & Other Stories

Diana is all set to welcome her loved ones for Christmas. An unexpected (and uninvited!) guest shows up at her door, spoiling her festive mood. All her attempts to thwart Dylan's intrusion go in vain as he keeps dropping in, again and again, insisting that she join his family for Christmas Eve dinner. Against her better judgment, she finally gives in, just to get him off her back. As they stand under the mistletoe after the dinner, Diana and Dylan know things have changed for the better for both.

A group of passengers is stranded at the airport together on New Year's Eve. Their plans were to celebrate the last day of the year and then ring in the new year with their loved ones by their side. But a delayed flight mars their plans and their happiness. They end up talking to each other, exchanging their New Year's Eve plans and how they celebrated it these many years so far. As they all welcome the new year together at midnight, their combined resolutions are to stay in touch with each other. They also resolve to make the best out of whatever life throws their way. Because as they have seen and experienced, not all things go as planned, always.

Samantha is visiting her native, Benakatti, after many years. Even though it's Christmas time, it's not a happy occasion in the family. As friends and family drop in for a visit, Samantha recalls the many winter breaks she spent in this village as a child. An unexpected guest shows up one day, bringing forth a cherished memory they had made on a foggy winter day many years ago.

These and 10 other stories encompass this festive special anthology. These are stories of hope, love, healing, new beginnings, acceptance, and everything that the holidays represent.

The Art of Being Grateful & Other Stories

Aashna receives a mysterious phone call in the middle of the night. The caller is a girl who says she has been kidnapped and will die if Aashna doesn't help her. Before Aashna can get details about the girl and her whereabouts, the phone gets cut off. Who was she and why did her voice sound eerily familiar? Will Aashna be able to help her?

Maanvi's life has always been about making everyone around realize that she is worthy too. From her test grades to her body type, everyone always had a piece of advice to give or some judgement to pass. How does Maanvi get affected by these? Does she manage to prove her worth to the world?

These and six other stories in this collection, cover a range of genres including romance, mystery, horror, thriller and much more. Delve in for a delightful reading journey!

The Untold Stories

Have you wondered about the events that happen around us? Do you think about the kind of lives people we come across everyday lead, and how they came to be what they are today? Our life is our story, but what about those little everyday incidents which create the anecdotes filling up the chapters of our life story? 'The Untold Stories' shares tiny anecdotes from people's everyday routines which go on to make remarkable chapters in their life stories. These anecdotes range from incidents around contemporary social issues and events such as terrorism and environmental imbalance to those circling around relationships.

A Rustic Mind

"We never think about the effects or repercussions of our everyday actions or even the things we come across on daily basis. Through 'A Rustic Mind' I aim to provide a thoughtful take on such actions and incidents. Poetic in its expression, these words will strike a chord which is not only deep but relatable on many levels. "

Ten Tales

This is a collection of short stories by authors across the world. The stories have been handpicked and selected based on their quality. The stories cover all genres in fiction.

Manali's story in this book is titled 'I'm Glad I'm Not Beautiful'. It spins a story around the much needed to be curbed issue and social stigma of acid attacks. The story circles around two school-going teenage girls, Abha and Vidhya, who are best friends, but are opposite in nature and appearance, and how a few incidents on a particular day turns their lives upside down.

Zista

"Zista represents Culture, the hub of which lies in India."

This title holds in its pages the very essence of India, its people and its culture, conveyed through a selection of short stories by few of the best authors of India.

Manali's story in this book is titled 'The Walls Have Ears'. This story helped her bag the Best Script Award. It talks about a young girl's day out in the infamous Kamathipura aka The Red-Light District of Mumbai.

Petrichor (compiled and edited by Manali Desai)

14 writers

7 short stories

9 poems

Who doesn't hold a special love for the rains? The smell of wet soil when the showers hit the surface of the Earth, opens up so much for us, emotionally. In this magical collection, we have some of the most special monsoon stories from a bunch of talented writers across the world. The contributors of this anthology traverse from 8 years old to 30 years old. What's common between them? Their love for monsoons of course! Because love for the rains is not age bound, right? This anthology is an attempt at bringing together writers from various walks of life. Each story or poem in this collection will make you rekindle your love with this most beloved season. It will be hard not to reminisce about your many romances with Indra over the years. The pages within this book will evoke nostalgic feelings in every reader. So, grab a cup of your favorite beverage and cozy up in your reading nook as you delve into Petrichor.

About the Author

Manali Desai

Manali is a full-time freelance writer and editor cum blogger. Currently, apart from her ad hoc writing and editing assignments, Manali runs a blog where she shares poetry, short fiction, book reviews, and personal stories. In her authoring journey, Manali has had nine books published under her name. Alongside that, she has also been a part of a few co-authored books (aka anthologies). Manali is a bestselling author on Amazon India with all her books ranking in the top ten in many categories. Her short story, The Walls Have Ears, helped her bag the Best Short Story Award in 2019 at Stories from India by Ukiyoto Publishing. She has also won the Best Author: Fiction Award at Cherry Books Awards, and the Book of The Year title in 2021 at BeTales Magazine Annual Awards, for her debut novel, Love (Try) Angle. Her short story titled, The (Un)Blind Date, which is a part of her Christmas special anthology, Under the Mistletoe & Other Stories, won the best story prize in an online contest by smitawritespen.com, before the book's release in December 2021. Her second novel, Love & (Mellow) Drama, was nominated for the prestigious AutHER Awards by Times of India in 2023. The same book also helped her win Best Author of the Year at Authoropod Magazine Annual Awards '23. You can find her on all socials as A Rustic Mind.

www.ingramcontent.com/pod-product-compliance
Lightning Source LLC
LaVergne TN
LVHW091534070526
838199LV00001B/62